For Doug, old
roomie, old friend,
Compañero de mi
Vida. Best always
Richard Hill

WHAT ROUGH BEAST?

Also by Richard Hill:

Ghost Story

Richard Hill

What Rough Beast?

A Foul Play Press Book

The Countryman Press, Inc.
Woodstock, Vermont

First Edition

Library of Congress Cataloging-in-Publication Data

Hill, Richard, 1941 Oct. 15—
What rough beast? / Richard Hill.
p. cm.
"A Foul Play Press book."
ISBN 0-88150-238-3 : $20.00
I. Title.
PS3558.I443W48 1992
813'.54—dc20 92-22036
CIP

A Foul Play Press Book
The Countryman Press, Inc.
Woodstock, Vermont 05091

Printed in the United States of America by Arcata Graphics

10 9 8 7 6 5 4 3 2 1

The author wishes to thank Jim Copp, US Army (Airborne); Fred Gress II, US Navy (SEAL); Sergeant Charles Zimmerman, USMC (all former); Agent Bill Porter, EOD, Arizona State Police; the guy at the Bullet Stop in Marietta, Georgia; and Col. Brown and the staff of SOF for technical assistance.

He is also grateful to the Ragdale Foundation, where he wrote some of this book, and the Virginia Center for the Creative Arts, where he finished it.

To the memory of Jim Morrison,
who knew something about bad
people on highways;

And for Eaddy, Julie, and Tommy:
Sweet memory lives!

WHAT ROUGH BEAST?

One

Autumn always does a job on me. It's a visceral sensation, a tug and shiver somewhere just inside the curve of my ribs. It weakens me, makes me nearly useless in the present. The first hint of cold wind seems to open me like some ragged scarecrow and I mourn—no matter how ugly—everything that was.

This year we got our first cold snap in early September. There was some color in the leaves already. The maples looked delicious in this early stage, like candy. In another month or two we'd have a full palette and the older tourists, or "leafers," would be among us, rubbernecking, weaving along these mountain roads at five or ten miles an hour, sometimes—in their rapture—driving off the road, past the barriers, and into the Callusaja Gorge.

I live just at the southern end of the Blue Ridge chain above a resort town called Highlands, North Carolina. I've lived here for a while, in relative peace and seclusion, making a living by way of an answering service, some yellow page ads, and a growing reputation as a private investigator who can find lost people. I try to take only cases in which finding a person would be good for somebody good or bad for somebody bad. It means traveling a lot, driving down into a world that doesn't show me much lately, but it beats anything else I've done, and it lets me live in the mountains.

In the winter we have the adolescent ski crowd, and in the summer we've got everybody from the old money gang at the Highlands Country Club to the Katels from Miami, whose deepest instincts seem to draw them every August to my land, where they park their motor home, unfold their chairs and card table, and sit, pink-kneed but hard-eyed behind Polarized sunglasses, daring me to make them move. Mr. Katel has threatened me several times with law suits for my objection to his trespass, so I've learned to be subtle.

This year I hired Verco Watkins, Jr., and two of his college friends to stand near the Katel RV in eight-hour shifts. Verco, Jr., is a bright young man and a psychology major at Western Carolina, but dressed in overalls and with a cheek full of Red Man, he looks like somebody from your worst *Deliverance* nightmare. He and his friends were creative. The one who took the first evening shift carried a stillborn baby pig. He had a way of talking and singing to himself to pass the night, a tremulous, nasal voice that carried to my cabin several times and troubled even *my* sleep. The Katels fired up the Winnebago at first light, Verco, Jr., had himself an interesting psych paper, and my land was free once more. Given a choice among the winter ski jerks, the Katels of summer, and the gentle, leaf-bemused older couples who come in the fall, I'll take the autumn leafers every time.

Most of the leafers were down in Florida now, nervously preparing for the season's first serious hurricane. I'd grown up there and had always liked hurricanes. Without storms, Florida weather would be an insufferable greenhouse hell, an endless turn of hot, breathless days and muggy, smothering nights—at its modern best, a life of air-conditioned malls and blistering asphalt. Without bad weather, Floridians would have no sense of the seasons, no way to measure and realize, despite the evidence all around them, that they were dying. Maybe that was what made it work, that and Ratso Rizzo's dream of easy living. "Two things are necessary to sustain life," Ratso had said in *Midnight Cowboy*. "Sunshine and coconut milk. In Florida you got both."

I wondered how strong a wind it would take to blow away all the plastic and restore something like the gritty paradise I remembered. I wondered how long it would take for them to build it back worse than before.

I have some friends who believe that life sends you what you need, the lessons you need to learn when you need to learn them. They assure me that the decade or so that I misspent underground was a karmic survival course for whoever it is that lives behind the things I do. Maybe they'd have said it was no accident that the phone rang that autumn day, and that I shouldn't have been surprised to hear—after nearly twenty years—the voice of Sarah Diehl.

It's eerie hearing a very familiar voice after that much time. Like a ghost. She didn't play guess-who games. "Randy, this is Sarah Diehl," she said, "Beth's sister." Voices don't change much. This one still had the flavor of a sixties sorority house. I was already a little haunted by the weather, so I stood there scarecrow-like and let the voice and the names it spoke rustle my straw some more.

Beth was my eleventh-grade girlfriend and Sarah went with my best friend, Happy. Those terms sound a little silly now, but what did we know? A year of double dates, beer, drive-ins, parking at the Indian mound and necking until our faces were raw, and a lot of laughs, good laughs, the kind innocent people have while they're learning to be worldly and not yet paying the world's price. The kind you have before you learn the cynical, braying college sneer and the brittle corporate snigger. The last of that kind of good laughter I had.

"Sarah, you called on the right kind of day."

"We're about to have a hurricane here," she said. "That's probably why I thought of you. I probably shouldn't be on the phone." I could hear a heavy back beat behind her voice.

"Is that a TV I hear?"

"My daughter's stereo."

"I can't hear you very well."

"Hang on." I heard voices behind the spacy static, then voices raised, then the stereo volume boosted to demonic level, then a slap and shout and silence, in which a door slammed. I heard her picking up the phone again. "God," she said, breathless, her voice shaky. "I'm sorry."

"No need. Talk to me. Tell me something good."

"Give me a minute." I heard ice cubes in a glass.

"I'll tell you something," I said. "The time we were having cookies and milk, trying to present your parents with a wholesome image when they came home, and Happy shook hands with your dad and when he did the long wigs opened up where he'd rigged them under his arms and fell out of his T-shirt like the world's longest underarm hair, and Beth laughed so hard milk came out of her nose. Good?"

"I need another one today. Hit me."

"Or when you worked in Dean Batten's office and stole that porn book from his file and gave it to me, and I was reading it behind my science text until Happy slipped Mr. Schoen a note to check what I was reading."

She laughed a little. "You refused to stand up."

"How could I do otherwise? My sap was rising. Part of me was already standing. Little Elvis was on stage."

She laughed better. "We were such jerks."

"We were like young gods," I said. "We were stardust, we were golden. We were going to build a new world. A bright new *fuuu*ture." I tried to imitate the Erpi Classroom Film announcer who'd fed us all the Brave New Disney World progress hype.

She didn't say anything for a while. My rhetorical excess had stalled and saddened me, too.

"What happened?" she asked.

"To me? To you?"

"To us. I wonder what happened to us, all of us. I've heard some scary stories about you. You were some kind of Navy commando. Then you were a cop. Then you were a very shady character in Atlanta. Then somebody told me you got sober. . . . My husband died of a heart attack."

She delivered that news with a rising inflection, almost like a question. I could hear her hands move on the receiver across all those miles. "I'm sorry," I said. "How's Beth?"

"Beth lost a son to a drunk driver. But we both still drink too much—though not if we're driving. We're neurotic as hell and unhappy in our golden chains, but Beth has a Ph.D. and the only marriage that lasted through the seventies, I'm rich, and you're . . . a detective?" A long pause. How much had she drunk today? Would this be one of those calls in which the party in pain is too numb to speak but too desperate to hang up? Or had our connection been broken? I decided just to wait. I wrote her name on my desk-top calendar, thinking I should have gotten her number in case this happened. "Yeah," she said finally, "I wonder in a general way about all of us. Our fall from . . . grace. I read a lot now, trying to figure things out. But most of all I wonder about Happy. Don't you?"

"Yes."

"Doesn't it bother you?" she asked.

"It always has," I said.

"I keep trying to make sense of it," she said. "What made him different from us? What decided that he'd be taken and we'd be spared?"

"We weren't spared," I said. "And we don't know that he was taken. Nobody gets out of here alive. Why worry about Happy?"

"But we do, don't we?" she said. "What's the last you heard?"

"That he came back from California for a while and was preaching Jesus to druggies on the beaches. I'd left town by then, so I didn't see him."

"Would you have gone to see him?"

"I don't know. Probably not. Did you?"

"Of course not. You didn't have to ask that. I'm the cute little rich girl in the ponytail. I went away to Sweet Briar. The drug beaches are off limits to people like me. The last taste I had of anything funky was with you and Happy and Beth in the Chevvy."

"We were just kidding around," I said. "Weren't we?"

"That's the *point*," she said. "We *were*. I thought we were. Then a big wave comes, and you're swept away and nearly go under, and Beth and I just barely survive our ordinary little dippy, sheltered lives, and Happy's *gone*, he's . . ."

Her silence upset me. "Maybe he's not gone," I said. "If the judge let him come back to Florida, it means he's O.K. there and didn't have any bad beefs out west."

"But Jesus," she said. "Not C.S. Lewis's Jesus or even Thomas Merton's Jesus, but the pamphleteering, glassy-eyed robot Jesus. Randy, was it drugs brought him to that? That's what people said. Too much *a*cid. Jesus!"

"Maybe. Lots of people find God that way. It's not my style of salvation either, but how do we know it's not what he wants and needs, assuming it wasn't a jailhouse conversion and he's still saved?"

"How do we know? Because you and I and Beth know he was as bright as anyone. It doesn't make sense for him to spend a year in jail on an assault charge, like some goddamn tattooed truck driver. I can't stand it. I want to know what happened."

"It's bothered me for a long time, too. I don't know why I haven't done something myself."

"It's what you do for a living, right?"

"Yes. I'm embarrassed."

"Well, I'm rich, and I want to hire you to find Happy and answer our questions, and if we can help him any way at all, do it. Come see me?"

"There's a hurricane down there. Bad moon a-risin'. Remember that song?"

"Yeah, and I remember you liked hurricanes. Remember our hurricane party the year Bertha came ashore? Christ!"

"Last I saw, that motel was still standing," I said. "At the end of Pass-a-grille. Storm knocked down all the power lines, took away the only bridge to St. Pete, and sank Capt. Michele's charter boat, along with its pier. Took us back a few years to when the ferry was the only way to get there and there were no such things as jet-skis and portable radios. Another storm like that and we'd see Pass-a-grille the way it was when the Timucuans speared mullet."

"You and Happy did an Indian dance to placate the storm. We watched you through that little bathroom window, knowing you'd be killed."

"We were drunk."

"But it worked," she said. "Come now, please."

"I'm coming," I said.

She gave me the address and number on Siesta Key. I heard the stereo again, louder than before. "What's your fee for corporal punishment of spoiled children?" she asked.

"Not my line. Dean Batten had that down, the last of his breed, I think. But you can do it, and I'll applaud."

"Sure you won't take a paddle to this girl?"

"That may be among the few things you can't hire folks to do for you," I said.

She didn't say anything and I listened to the noise for a while. Finally she said goodbye and hung up. I wished we'd ended better, but we'd have another chance.

Two

I asked Verco Watkins, Sr., to watch my cabin and take care of my husky, Jack. I took 441 at Clayton, Georgia, and cut over to I-75 north of Macon. I hated to miss Last Supper Recaps, but I wanted a big road in and out of Florida. There's a little town on 221 just north of Valdosta where somebody painted a very poor but sincere rendition of the da Vinci work on a building that also houses a used-tire and recap exchange. The result is what looks like Last Supper Tires—with Jesus and the boys looking down in a kindly way upon a splinter-edged wood door frame and piles of ragged rubber—and I usually drive a few miles out of my way for the mental and spiritual refreshment it brings me.

But 221 is a lonely, winding, old-fashioned road, and I wanted to see what was happening on the interstate. About the only thing heading south besides me was a bag of McDonald's McLitter duckwalking along the median, pushed by the wind. Traffic was stacked up in the northbound lanes, tourists fleeing the storm. It looked like the end of the world and I loved it.

I thought about staying in a motel, but I hate motels. The expensive ones were already filled with fleeing Yankees running around like extras in an Irwin Allen movie, and the one I checked in Valdosta had walls so thin you could see the maid's silhouette as she rotated the sheets next door. I decided to stay on the road and just pull over if I dozed.

I got the salad bar and some hot tea at a truck stop. Somebody played "Amazing Grace" on the jukebox and reminded me once again that my father's Latin sensibilities have never dominated my mother's cracker blood for long.

And I had the blues. When they come, they come. There's no predicting and no preventing them. Maybe it was the weather, and talking about old times, and the sight of cypress hammocks and Spanish moss and being the only man heading my way on one of the world's busiest interstates. Maybe it was being the age I was, over forty with more than a decade of that life spent in ways I should probably be grateful I forgot. Maybe it was that bad life calling me back, what my sober friends call a dry drunk. Maybe the geek who lived inside me was thirsty. Or maybe it was just my time to have the blues, like a cold. It wasn't exactly the lowdown, dragass, whaleshit, hope-to-die blues I had, but a form of almost pleasant melancholy—a reverie, weakness, sweet sadness.

I tried to find some blues on the radio—hair of the dog that bit me—but it was all either hurricane bulletins or country or echohead DJs and Top 40 tunes that all sound the same.

The sky darkened as I drove into Florida. There wasn't much point in driving straight through and waking Sarah in the middle of the night, so I pulled in to a rest area. There were no other cars there, so I was surprised to see a man standing before the big map and bulletin board on the wall between the restrooms. I didn't make a lot of noise approaching, but I assumed he heard me. The closer I got, the stranger it seemed for him to be there. I stopped before I reached the concrete and watched him.

I realized that he wasn't aware of me. His eyes were fixed on something beneath the glass of the bulletin board. I couldn't make it out from where I stood.

I heard a noise, a breathy shuddering moan. He shivered now and then, although the wind was humid and warmed by the Gulf it was churning to the west. He pressed his hands together in a prayerful way, just touching his chin and lower lip with the tips of his fingers. His body bent periodically as if responding to a chill, pain, or some odd sort of sexual arousal. He was about 5' 11" and wiry, in his early or mid-thirties. He wore khaki pants, desert boots, and a London Fog type of windbreaker. He was clean shaven, with almost crew-cut, dark-blond hair, and rather neatly dressed—like a preppie hiker you might find in an L.L. Bean catalog. But the preppie in the Bean catalog wouldn't make these noises, wouldn't reach up to touch the glass that protected the poster, wouldn't reach down to touch himself between his legs.

I cleared my throat. He seemed only faintly to register the sound. "Hello," I said.

He ducked first, twisting his body. He almost fell, then ran, taking as much room to pass me as he could. He continued running, slipped on the wet grass, then scrambled up and ran on through the wind and gusts of rain, past the drinking fountain and dog walk sign, across our empty southbound lanes of I-75, and into the busy northbound lanes. I heard brakes lock and tires moan and slide on the wet pavement, a horn sound and miraculously no collisions.

Should I follow? The wind gusted, then died for a few seconds, then came up again and made me shiver. The rest area on the northbound side was crowded with refugees. I wasn't sure I could even find him if I did make it through the traffic. And why should I chase him? I wasn't even sure what he'd been doing here, why he'd apparently parked across the highway and come here to view this bulletin board in his strange, private way.

What did I remember? His body, trembling, rigid before the bulletin board. His sudden moves, like an animal in a net. His eyes as he passed me. Most of all his eyes. His eyes were gone. They saw things I couldn't.

I walked back to look at what had so moved him. It was a poster showing the photographs of two rather zaftig young women and offering a reward for information leading to the capture of person or persons who had come upon their tent in the Hillsborough State Park north of Tampa and raped, stabbed repeatedly, and decapitated them. It gave the name and number of a Hillsborough County detective.

I didn't hesitate. I called it. I've only had this feeling a few times, and I don't question it when it comes. My scrotum crawls and tries to creep up into my body; I feel a tingle and a weakness along my ribs and behind my arms and legs, and a great sadness and emptiness inside. It's how cold-blooded murder feels—not what you *think* about it but how it *feels*.

It's how I felt when I saw a blond merchant seaman stomp a Cuban pimp in pre-Fidel Havana. I was a little kid. My Uncle Gabe had gotten drunk and nostalgic and bought us both tickets, and I'd gone without telling my folks. I guess he thought he'd teach me about our home island and advance my worldly education. He did. The stomping went on and on, longer than anybody expected and certainly longer than necessary. The sounds changed as the larger bones gave way. Blood spread to the curb and flowed into the gutter. Uncle Gabe was sick on the sidewalk; it was then I knew it must be real. The reality of it reached the seaman last, and he withdrew with a clumsy, numb kind of distaste. All in an open café on a busy street with four Batista cops looking on. When the seaman walked away in a berserker daze, the cops resumed an earlier conversation. The pimp looked like somebody who'd fallen to the street from an airplane.

I didn't have words for it then but I remember it all clearly, and I'll never forget the feeling. It's the touch of death's cold finger upon our so-fragile lives, Moloch's gamey breath in our nostrils. I knew I'd seen the man who killed the girls.

Detective Lieutenant Romanello was interested, though naturally cautious. I told him who I was, what I was doing in Florida, and what I'd seen. Who I was included the period I'd worked for Sheriff Hubbard in his county. I'd worn the same uniform, although I'd been undercover and hadn't worn it much. Sheriff Hubbard, we both knew, was enjoying a rather splendid retirement in the Bahamas, from which distance he had recommended me, more or less accurately, for my North Carolina P.I. ticket. Most of us liked Sheriff Hubbard, although we wouldn't want to talk about him under oath.

I gave Romanello the best description I could and Sarah's number. Romanello said he'd like to talk with me again and would I try to come by, weather permitting, and describe him for a sketch artist. He said he'd put out the word, but that without a vehicle description and considering the hurricane exodus, there didn't seem to be much hope of catching him before the state line. Not catching him, of course, so much as asking him to come in and answer a few questions. After all, we had not a shred of evidence. He thanked me.

I called Sarah and told her I was stopping for the night. She gave me directions and told me what shelter she'd be in if the storm moved closer and she had to evacuate. I knew she was afraid of the storm, but her voice told me she might prefer having the wind blow the whole Gulf through her condo to spending the night on a cot in a high school gym filled with portable radios and hysterical Katelites. I knew how she felt.

I left the rest area and found an exit farther south which led me to a cluster of convenience stores and gas stations, all but one closed. The wind seemed higher now, with occasional gusts that made me fight for balance as I filled my tank. I asked the boy who took my money if there were a place I could park and sleep. I told him I had a sick relative in St. Pete and had to be there but was too sleepy to drive any farther. He told me to park behind his brother-in-law's junk yard down the road. It was doubtful anyone could see me and once he talked nice to the Dobermans they stopped barking at me. I thanked him. I was glad the Dobermans were nearby to warn me if I had visitors.

I rigged the Eagle wagon for sleeping, which was mainly a matter of putting my luggage up front, lowering the rear seat-back, and rolling out my piece of foam and sleeping bag. As it happened I had four pistols with me and a good deal of ammunition. I had my older 9mm Browning and a Colt Government .45, a Brazilian Taurus 9mm and a Smith and Wesson stainless .357 Magnum revolver. I also had the pointed tire tool, the handcuffs, and the K-Bar diver's combat knife I usually carry in the car. I wasn't packing all the guns because I thought I'd need them, but because if the weather let up I wanted to spend some time with my old gunsmith friend, Robbie, in Clearwater. I wanted to do some shooting and have him do some sighting and other modifications to the pistols.

So if the dogs warned me in time I had plenty of firepower, and I felt silly. I figured the guy I'd spooked and who was now spooking me was in Georgia by now. Nonetheless, I put the other pieces the legal two moves away—in the glove compartment and under the front seat—and slept with the Colt cocked and locked. The wind and rain were an almost steady white noise now, and I liked it. I realized I'd lost my blues; real trouble often has that effect. The next thing I knew, the Dobermans were barking and although the sky was still dark, I knew it was morning.

I listened to the radio while I warmed up the car and rolled up my sleeping gear. There was more rain in the wind. The radio said that the hurricane was stalled in the Gulf about a hundred miles west of Tampa Bay, where it had been stationary for over eighteen hours. The dogs were barking at their owner, who'd been told I'd be there and gave me a wave as he walked the yard, checking to see if there'd been any storm damage so far to his junk cars. The Dobies rubbed against his legs like housecats.

There was nothing on the radio about the murders, but they'd happened almost a month ago and couldn't compete with the storm. I wondered that I hadn't heard about them, except that I do live in a certain degree of isolation, and despite my dish antenna and VCR, I can go on a two- or three-day hike in these days of media blitz and miss a small war. By the time I get back and reattach myself to the glass teat, everybody else has fought it, commented on it, and forgotten it.

I bought the best breakfast I could from a bank of machines in my benefactor's station. It wasn't easy. I found some orange juice and a granola bar that wasn't covered with chocolate. I washed up in the restroom and my friend brought me some real paper towels. The old service station courtesies are not quite dead.

I drove on south to Tampa and decided to see Romanello first. I passed the old garage on I-75 north of the dog track on which, in the Sixties, when I was in college there, someone had painted ROCK AND ROLL and a peace sign. It was still there, and probably a few innocents still expected its magic to take effect some day. Woodstock Nation—a message from the mystical past for the fourteen-year-old kid next door who's just smoked his first crack and knows he'll never have to feel fourteen again.

The sheriff's offices were just off the interstate. Everybody was busy with the storm, but I found Romanello and we talked a little while we waited for the sketch artist. He said the FBI wanted to see the sketch, but had a lot of reservations about my hunch. I shrugged. I didn't blame them. He also told me that rape, stabbing, mutilation, and decapitation were not, according to the coroner, necessarily the exact order of the crimes. I asked him how it was possible to tell, and he said only if the sexual abuse came some time after the victim's death, and we both made the kinds of faces hard guys make when they hear things like that. Romanello asked me if I wanted to know more; I told him I had a case of my own and would just as soon not know what I already did about his.

When the artist came, I did my best, and he did his best, and we looked at it. Maybe it would help narrow the search some, but I never really trusted that technique. I've never seen anybody who looked like a police sketch, except maybe this guy. But then I couldn't describe him well enough to help the artist realize that he *did* look like a police sketch. He was the guy sipping coffee on the next stool, in front of you at the bank, driving alongside you on the freeway, observing the speed limit. He didn't stick in your mind's eye. He blended in, even alone there on the interstate. In Dick Tracy he would probably have been called "Anyface." Was that what chilled me? If the killer could have been almost any of us, did it follow that almost any of us could be the killer?

Maybe he was some kind of psychotic chameleon mutation—call it the Bundy Syndrome—that carried his poison, not in a scarred body marked with jailhouse tattoos, but in the boy next door. Maybe his ordinariness, his nondistinction, was somehow the *source* of his poison. He was the tail-wagging pup you stopped to pet who then went for your throat. All you saw were those few seconds of deadly truth, the truth I had seen in his eyes the moment he turned. Without that, without the look that made my balls try to hide, he looked like a million harmless white guys.

Romanello was a big man with a very heavy beard and dark circles around his eyes, one of those jocks who reach a certain age and can't keep the same weight and still work at a job that makes it hard not to drink too much—all of which probably describes the classic American male. It was lunch time and he was buying.

He took me to a place not far from the stadium where we could get a Cuban sandwich and bean soup and Cuban coffee—the real stuff from my daddy's life. Romanello ordered two vodka martinis in case the bar waitress got busy, and I told him I'd had to quit a few years back. He shook his head sadly that such a thing should ever become necessary, and lit another low-tar cigarette. There wasn't much chance of the bar waitress being busy. The storm had fixed it so we pretty much had the place to ourselves, and a waiter had just put up a sign saying they'd be closing for the duration in another hour. I told Romanello that my father was a second-generation Ybor City Cuban-American who had met my mom at a dance at the Vinoy Hotel in St. Pete the night she and her sisters arrived from Kentucky in a Model T. I was born in Tampa, but mom later talked dad into moving to St. Pete.

"The name on your PI ticket is Randall Gatsby Sierra," he said. "Want to explain that?"

"I don't mind. My old man was a big fan of F. Scott Fitzgerald."

"Mine was a big fan of Al Capone," Romanello said. "Probably why I'm a cop." He told me he was from one of those old Tampa Italian families which for generations had shared the power—legal and illegal—with the Cubans and Anglos. He'd rebelled and spent his youth in the California Highway Patrol, then had come home to what he'd hoped would be a quieter life. I asked him not to smoke while we ate what for me was a special lunch. When the coffee came he fired up another low tar, the kind that have the little peace sign in their filters and smell like a wet dog too close to a space heater.

He told me there was now a back way to Sarasota, an extension of I-75 that ran east of Tampa and Hillsborough Bays and avoided St. Pete altogether. I thanked him, we shook hands, and I took his directions. I also found on the far left of the dial a radio station that was run by its listeners in something like the old progressive format, and they were playing some blues. I listened to some Mississippi John Hurt, some Sonny Boy Williamson Number Two, some Joe Williams with Basie's big band, and to a white New Orleans bluesman named Spencer Bohren. I drove through what the wind hadn't blown away of the phosphate dust and petro smog and the trailer parks and topless bars (one called Strip Ahoy) of a short and sad back bayside Redneck Riviera to a point where, finally, it was open road and palmettos and pine, and, for a few miles, I could taste my youth.

Our youth. Now Sarah lived on Siesta Key, with artists, writers, investors in the market. I found it after a while. There was a cute and quaint little village shopping center where the road met the Gulf and turned north. I remembered a couple of lost weekends I'd spent here with artists and writers and investors in various kinds of markets. I called from a phone booth and she gave me the more precise directions. She sounded nervous. "I expected you sooner," she said. "Did you have an interesting trip?"

I assured her that I had.

Three

Sarah had cut off her long, blond hair. I don't know why I expected a ponytail, but I was disappointed. She had a stylish, short haircut that somehow suggested both money and institutional care. The sun had bleached it and given her one of those careless leisure tans you don't duplicate on a two-week vacation. We gave each other a cautious hug. I could hear Wagner from a far room. Her body felt thin through the loose, shapeless beach dress. Not thin so much as insubstantial, fragile. Her eyes looked as if they'd been carrying some literal weight. She'd found the right man and lost him.

She turned away and I followed her to her living room and its view of the Gulf in its most dangerous mood. "I got a man to board up the windows," she said, "except for that one. He said to nail this plywood over it from the inside if things got worse. They don't get worse. They don't get better. At least we're on the second floor. Would you like a drink . . . of something?"

"What I'd really like first is a shower and a shave. I thought I'd try a motel."

She smiled for the first time. "They have all fled. We are here abandoned to nature's fury." It was a thing the four of us used to do—try to talk like poems, like rhymed couplets or blank verse.

"Blow, wind, rack your cheeks," I said.

"It's *crack* your cheeks, doofus," she said.

"Blow, wind, crack your cheeks, doofus," I said.

She laughed, and gave me the rest: "'Rage! Blow! You cataracts and hurricanoes, spout till you have drench'd our steeples, drown'd the cocks! You sulph'rous and thought-executing fires, vaunt-couriers of oak-cleaving thunderbolts, singe my white head! And thou, all-shaking thunder, strike flat the thick rotundity o' th' world! Crack nature's molds, all germins spill at once that makes ingrateful man!' . . . I think your line now is 'Here's a night pities neither wise men nor fools.'"

We gave each other a better hug. "It sure has been a long time," I said.

"Go get your luggage," she said. "Then take a nice shower. I have some things to show you."

I found a closer parking space for the Eagle. Most of her condo neighbors had clearly headed for higher ground and I had my choice. I saw a British Racing Green Jag sedan and a little red Audi Fox parked together near Sarah's end of the building and figured they were hers. Even in a storm, you could smell the money here. Her condo was the last in the row, directly on the beach. I didn't know what the cost was on a living situation like that, but I knew I'd never have it. If I ever did, I knew I'd spend it on a piece of Idaho or Oregon or British Columbia or New Zealand a lot bigger than what I could afford here.

I put the .45 into my suitcase and the rest of my pieces into a duffel bag I carried for shoes and laundry. I figured it'd be smarter to drag everything up to Sarah's second-floor rooms, in case it flooded. It was blustery outside, but really no worse than it had been all day. This storm was named David, but David, so far, was a tease.

Sarah showed me to a room—the only bedroom directly on the Gulf—and its welcome shower. As I closed the door, the Valkyries tangled with some modern shrieking and a nasty, whip-crack, synthesized backbeat. I'd forgotten about the kid. When I'd dried off and dressed, I joined Sarah in the living room. The daughter's stereo was still thumping but she'd joined her mom. She had the same kind of haircut and tan and looked at me the way a cat will when you've just met. Her arms were crossed but not her legs. Since she occupied a chaise longue directly across from the couch where Sarah and I sat, and since she was wearing the same kind of beach dress, only shorter and riding higher on her thighs, there was a problem of which her mother and I became aware at about the same time.

"Dammit, Jennifer," Sarah said. "Are you wearing any pants?"

Jennifer was indignant and coy at the same time. "Jesus, Mother, you told me to make him welcome."

"You didn't answer my question." Sarah's voice had the exhausted tone of the modern, whine-worn parent. Her eyes moved around the room, making no contact with her daughter.

Jennifer never answered the question. She pulled her dress down and said that she was happy to meet me. She shifted her body language and tone of voice and was suddenly and briefly another person, a polite and interested young lady. "Mother tells me you're old friends. She says you're hip. I think she means you did a lot of drugs and know something about music."

"I don't think that's what she meant at all," I said. "I think I used to be hip. I sure tried. I don't think I'm hip any more. It's a real burden."

"Huey Lewis," she said, putting the idea and me into a pop pigeonhole. Maybe we belonged there. Jennifer and I weren't going to get along, and I didn't care. I was tired of trying to understand adolescents, tired of a world that spent so much time trying to amuse them and separate them from their parents' money, tired of the concept of adolescence—an invention of modern psychologists and marketing wizards. For centuries people had been young for a while and then taken on their adult responsibilities, brutal as both youth and adulthood may have been. Now we had carved out a never-never-land of irresponsibility and conspicuous, noisy consumption that seemed to expand every year, reaching backward into childhood and forward into what had been maturity until we were all teenagers—boisterous and insecure, arrogant and whiny, punching up and trying out personalities the way kids flip channels with a remote control.

Jennifer closed one eye and cocked her head at me as if she were considering what I'd said about the burden of hipness. She was wearing what looked to be a very expensive watch on a lavender suede band. Or maybe it was mauve. I'm not too sure about the subtler colors. Otherwise, she was unadorned and casual. She was about sixteen or seventeen, with a coltish body like her mother's at that age. "Do you think it's fair for her to play her music and I can't play mine?" she asked me.

"I've gotten to the point that I don't even like music much any more," I said. I was baiting her now. "I think there's entirely too much music around, too many people singing, playing guitars, writing songs. I'd just as soon sit here and listen to the wind. You don't get a hurricane every day. Why can't we just talk and listen to the wind?"

"Listen, hell," Jennifer said. "Mother's *keeping* us here where we're probably going to get *killed*." She took advantage of our slow response to rise and walk into the den. The Valkyries died in mid-shriek. Sarah's jaw muscles clenched. Jennifer returned without even a glance at her mother and rearranged herself on the chaise.

"Jennifer wants to visit her friend, Cissy, in Orlando," Sarah said, her voice metallic. "Cissy's parents are having a party for all the poor orphans of the storm from this coast. All the spoiled brats with designer watches and German cars are to be consoled at one of the Disney World hotels. Someone must make up to them for this awful, windy inconvenience."

Jennifer heard the snap in Sarah's voice and decided on a temporary silence. Sarah wasn't finished. "Jennifer can't make up her mind whether she wants to be Nancy Reagan, Madonna, Joan of Arc, or Mother Jones when she grows up," she said, her voice tighter and higher than she probably intended. "*If* she lives long enough for it to be said, by anyone, that she has, in fact, *grown up*."

Jennifer let a few beats go by, then took the tone of someone placating a dangerous mental patient.

"Mother, may I see the things you were going to show Mr. Sierra? We could share some family memories."

Sarah rose and left us, walking stiffly. After a while, Jennifer's stereo stopped.

"Mother thinks I'm a Top 40 twit-twat," Jennifer said in a confidential tone. "I read books. I like Camus. I'm interested in serious music. Stuff you can't hear on the radio around here. Music can change the world."

"We thought music would change the world, too," I said. "I'm afraid it did."

Jennifer tried to pretend I was joking. We both played at being friendly, sophisticated adults, and I warmed up to her a little. Sarah called me, and Jennifer gave me a look that suggested we try to be a little tolerant of her mom's eccentricity.

I heard something new from Sarah's stereo. It had to be an old 45 of Richie Valens' "La Bamba." It wasn't the new Los Lobos version. "Mom plays that sometimes," Jennifer said. "I think it's great."

I went to help Sarah with a steamer trunk she was trying to haul from a walk-in closet in her bedroom. Once she saw I had it well in hand, she said: "I'm going to make another drink. Probably a Brompton's Cocktail. Or maybe a Molotov Cocktail. No, I think I'll just have a water glass full of crushed ice and vodka."

I carried the trunk to the foot of the couch and set it down. Jennifer gave me a conspiratorial and coy look. "Strong," she said. "Are you going to be sleepin' in there tonight?" I heard ice being crushed in the kitchen.

"Listen, kid," I said. "While your mother's gone let me explain myself to you. I'm not a subtle guy. I'm hardly even civilized. I've probably got less patience than anyone you've ever met for this kind of sick family theater. So why don't you put on your happy-child face for the rest of the evening. That way I don't feed you one of these pillows."

Her perfect tan slipped a few notches, and I felt like a bully. Richie Valens finished and the needle moved back to start again. She decided to believe me, but she tried one more shot. "It's because I'm sixteen," she said.

"No," I said. "It's because you're a pain in the ass."

She made an amazing recovery before Sarah got the drink made and returned to us, and by the time we opened the trunk you'd have thought it was her birthday. She stayed that way for the rest of the evening, or as much of it as we spent together. "La Bamba" took a few more encores. Finally Sarah went over and moved the arm and let the music die.

Much of what Sarah had was family photos, so there was a good deal of sorting to do. She showed me her husband. He was a good-looking man and I said I thought so. Jennifer smiled. She seemed to be really enjoying herself—free, by virtue of my dire threat, to be a sixteen-year-old version of her radical bad self. She was delightful. Even Sarah was charmed. We passed through photos of the still-mourned dead and dug our way downward through Jennifer's time toward the images of our high school daze and Sarah, Beth, Happy, and me before we knew enough to be afraid and sad.

Sometimes I think there's more of us in photos than in real life. I guess photographers think so all the time. In real life we have body language, tone of voice, and the expectations and moods of the people around us to hide behind. Even the dopiest family snapshot shows, for that instant, a naked human. What had Happy looked like? I wasn't sure what to expect. We passed the photos among ourselves. Happy was smiling in most of them. I was more often the serious one. I was surprised at his innocence. Cocky, sure, but just another playful kid growing up, struggling with his testosterone. He had a long and pointed face and a prominent nose, like one of the smaller predators—like a fox, in fact, or a weasel. In the beach pictures he displayed a medium frame and wiry body, knobby with muscle, like Popeye's.

We found Sarah's ponytail. She had kept it in a plastic bag. Jennifer asked to see it and touched it with what looked like genuine affection. There were clips from the school paper. Cupid's Arrow had struck Sarah Diehl and Happy Fox, rumor had it, during the weekend drag finals at Brooksville. There were photos of both lovestruck teens.

"Drags?" I said. "Did we do that?" Jennifer looked to her mom for an answer.

"Are you kidding? It was your car we raced. I still think it was what ruined my hearing."

"It was my stereo, Mom," Jennifer said.

"And the Valkyries," Sarah offered. Jennifer gave her mother a gentle and playful punch.

"But drag racing is blue-collar, dirty-knuckle, white-trash stuff," I said. "Or at least it was then."

"What do you think you guys were," Sarah asked, "a couple of preppies from Choate?"

"I like to think I was welcome in the best homes," I said.

"Mostly after midnight through the window or when the parents were out," Sarah said.

"So you guys were like punks?" Jennifer asked. I hesitated, trying to see if she was in a role, if she was condescending to play the interested teen. It seemed genuine. She seemed to have forgotten that she was pretending to be good.

"It was left over from *Blackboard Jungle*," I said, embarrassed. "It was our pale, southern resort-town imitation of big city hardass. The Beatles hadn't been around long enough to mellow us."

"Yeah, pale, resort-town imitation," Sarah said. "Check these guys." There we were. It was a newspaper photo of a fight outside the Sugar Shack after school. I had no idea who'd have taken it, maybe some freelance who just happened along. Some guys had driven down from Piney Park to see a girl they'd met at a dance, a girl who went to our school. We had apparently taken offense. The cops had just arrived. The old cop had his billy raised above Happy's head. Happy was on a guy's chest. The guy was lying on his back. I was hanging on to the neck of a big kid with very greasy hair. Both my feet were off the ground, and there was a young cop gripping the waist of my jeans.

There was a ring of punks around the action: I saw Junior Huddle's elfin figure, his black hair gleaming. I saw Aldo Rizzo's giant head and slightly open-mouthed smirk above his powerful, squat body and short legs. I saw Petey Pollard's handsome, blond head wreathed in the smoke from his dangling cigarette. They were holding back the crowd. The caption read GANG VIOLENCE FLARES.

I was embarrassed. I identified with all the souls the camera had caught that day but the one that was supposed to be mine. I stole a glance at Jennifer, who registered my chagrin but withheld comment.

"I'd forgotten about that," I mused. "We were just . . . I think we were just . . . . "

"Acting?" Jennifer said, with a slight smile. "Maybe you were just trying out different adult roles while you were still kids and before you grew up and had to be one for the rest of your life."

Sarah saved me from having to answer her daughter. "It was very strange," she said, having missed most of the business between Jennifer and me and still gazing at the old newsclip. Happy had written on it: "The Boys." Sarah continued: "Most of those guys were from homes and backgrounds that fitted this kind of behavior. They'd do this kind of thing for a few years until they either were graduated from high school or dropped out to take blue-collar jobs or went to jail. Some had potential to get out, but couldn't overcome their social disadvantages. At least that was the sociological cant at the time. Petey Pollard was a sweet boy, once you got to know him. But even Petey belonged in this picture. I never thought that Randy and Happy did."

"But we're the ones doing the fighting," I said.

"Yeah, you did it sometimes, but you also got pretty good grades, and you both knew how to dress when you had to, and you could talk to parents like gentlemen. You both read books. You and Happy could go back and forth across that line. Beth and I figured you would both choose eventually to stay on our side. Our parents didn't have that kind of confidence or hope. For the most part they were right. Both of you got caught on that side and Happy never did get back."

"But we read Shakespeare together. Remember when we did *Romeo and Juliet* for your folks?"

"*West Side Story* might have been more appropriate," Sarah said. "'When you're a Jet you're a Jet all the way.'"

"'From your first cigarette to your last dying day'," Jennifer offered, surprising me again.

Sarah lit another cigarette. "There must be a line people cross," she continued, almost as if musing alone. "At some point in his life, an individual does something or neglects to do something and at that moment all the playacting is over and most of his options are closed. You and Happy gave the impression that you'd beat that system, have it both ways, keep your choices open. I think a lot of us hoped you would. Maybe we only *think* we have options. Maybe nobody has that much choice."

She pulled out a folded piece of newsprint and opened it. There was Happy's face, glaring at the police camera and the world. It was the face of the classic sociopath. The story was about his assault on a man during a traffic fracas. He'd attacked the man—an attorney as it turned out—then followed him to the Mound Park emergency room and jumped him again. He'd beaten him unconscious, then jumped a hospital security guard who'd made the mistake of coming out to stop the fight without his weapon. The guard was rescued by a pair of city cops who came with their weapons drawn and took Happy away in handcuffs. He was given a year in the city jail for assault—the longest city-jail sentence ever handed down.

"What happened?" Jennifer asked. "Why did he get so weird?"

"That's what I want Randy to find out," Sarah said. "There's only one thing I remember, something very vivid still that might be part of the explanation. You remember his dad."

I nodded. "Drank a lot. Tended bar sometimes. Never seemed to be around much. Little, pale guy. Quiet."

"But once he hit Happy's mom. Several times. I guess he'd knocked her down and she was on the floor when Happy came in."

"He never told me about it."

"Maybe I'm the only one he told," Sarah said. "He beat his father. His mother tried to stop him, but he couldn't stop, at least for a while. His mother scratched and hit him trying to pull him off his dad. Finally Happy started crying and left his dad alone. His mother put iodine and Band-aids and ice on his dad, then Happy tried to do the same for her. Everybody was crying by then. His dad went out. Happy came over here, or to my parents' house. He was still crying off and on, still angry. We talked for a long time. When my dad made me come in, he drove down to the Indian mound and slept in his car. That's the last time I saw him when he wasn't tough."

Sarah stopped and stared at her drink. I wasn't sure she knew we were there. Then she looked up. "Maybe it's not too late to help him." She turned to Jennifer. "Or would it embarrass you to have it known we were helping somebody like that?"

Jennifer looked genuinely hurt. She stood and left us without a word. We heard her door close.

"Let's see what the radio says," Sarah suggested. "If it's safe I'd like to go out for something to eat. I don't think I can do any more harm here for a while." She sank into the cushions with a sigh, gathering her strength. Jennifer's door opened again and she came back through the den and leaned into the living room.

"I'm sorry, Jenny," Sarah said.

"It's O.K. If you're going out to eat, would you bring me something?"

"Sure. I want to see if Jean-Pierre is open. Otherwise we'll have to take our chances on the mainland."

"The *steak au poivre,*" said Jennifer. "Thanks."

"Would you like to come with us?" I asked, trying to be good myself.

"No, thanks," Jennifer said with a martyr's smugness. "You and Mom have a lot to talk about. Good to meet you."

"Same here," I said.

"By the way," she said, "I was wearing pants." Jennifer

laughed. I laughed. Finally Sarah joined us. We were silly, and it was a blessing that we could all know it.

Four

We found a tired but excited TV weather man who told us that Hurricane David had moved to the north and west a few degrees, then stalled again. There might be some slight relief from the wind in our area, but we were not, repeat, not safe. We should continue to take all the advised precautions.

Sarah called Jean-Pierre and learned that he was open. Jean-Pierre, she told me, was a Frenchman and anarchist/socialist from Martinique, a man who claimed to have hurricane experience. He would make his own decisions about whether or not to open La Grenouille. I asked her how a man of his political convictions felt about serving food to rich capitalists. "I think he loves it," she said. "He preaches a lot. The food's so good that they listen, or pretend to. Maybe they accept Jean-Pierre as their conscience. I may be the only customer who ever agrees with him."

"A parlor pink, eh?"

"I'm afraid so. Or at least an old-fashioned liberal. Come the revolution my little portfolio's going to be in big trouble."

She let me drive the Jag. Just smelling it made me feel I belonged on Siesta Key. On the way to La Grenouille,

Sarah showed me John D. MacDonald's house. There seemed to be nobody home. "I thought you'd like to see where Travis McGee hailed from," she said. "I guess they've gone inland like everybody else with any sense."

There seemed at first to be nobody home at the restaurant. Then we heard a loud, French voice and a tall, thin man came out to kiss Sarah and peer at me suspiciously.

"Jean-Pierre, this is Randall Gatsby Sierra, a friend of my youth. He's a private investigator and Wobbly sympathizer."

Jean-Pierre looked back and forth between us, waiting for a cue. "You are joking with me?"

"I came along too late, of course," I said. "I was an English major once. I was still writing to Sarah and her sister then. I got interested in Dos Passos, wrote papers on him, Bill Haywood, Gene Debs, Joe Hill, John Reed. Sarah was exaggerating."

"Did you read Dos Passos's late work?" Jean-Pierre demanded. "Why do so many of them turn into crusty old reactionaries? I think he even lived long enough to approve of Reagan, a man best suited by intellect and temperament to be a caddy."

"I don't know why," I said.

"It is very good to meet you nonetheless," he said. "Our menu is somewhat limited tonight by the absence of fresh seafood. Let me bring you a glass of something—here, first, I light your candle. You will have, I expect, my full attention tonight."

"Perhaps you'll join us for a drink," I said.

"I thank you very much, but I think not. I am cooking all alone tonight, my wife having taken all the living things of my household to a place called Ocala. And I suspect that you will wish to talk of the time since last you met. What for you?"

"Nothing for me. A glass of soda. Perrier, maybe."

He made a face. Sarah ordered a glass of Cabernet. We

decided on veal and ordered something to go for Jennifer.

Jean-Pierre was a very good cook, under any circumstances. We ate; we listened to the wind against the restaurant; we talked.

"I don't think Jennifer's a bad human being," she said. "But she's done some very irresponsible things. She's had a terrible time with drugs already. She's clean now, but when she used, she seemed to have no judgment about how much, how long. She nearly died. Can you imagine a fifteen-year-old debutante free-basing cocaine? I know it has something to do with losing her father. Gary says—"

"Gary?"

"Her therapist. He says she's still dealing with the loss of her father."

"I don't doubt that," I said. "But children have always lost fathers. Always will. We lost ours. I guess we got loaded, too, but . . . we were older."

"What makes them different from us? *Are* they different?"

"I've looked for a lot of runaways. In some ways the problem's a perennial one. In other ways, there's never been anything like it in the history of the world. Nobody's ever had stronger drugs, more variety, more availability. Nobody ever. They're cheap, strong, and you can buy them at school, at the mall, the beach. Nobody any age can handle some of those drugs."

"But even kids who aren't on drugs seem . . . different."

"They're probably not that different from us, but they live in a different world. In this way they're like us: The typical adolescent, then and now, wants two things—one, absolute stability, two, total anarchy. I've thought about that a lot, and that describes my adolescence, and I'd guess hers, too. But, they're growing up in a different world. They're trained from childhood to need radio, TV,

Top 40, MTV. They try to live in a TV commercial and it doesn't measure up so they get high. It's *Brave New World* right here in River City."

"But they have parents . . . ."

"Their parents are afraid of them. Lots of parents have the same values as their kids. They *talk* like their kids—ever notice? A lot of these parents were reared the same way, by parents with little paperback books in their hands and in schools that stressed creativity. It didn't work. Those were wonderful ideas for kids who were already born or trained to be cooperative, but for the majority they failed. We kept asking the kids what they wanted to do and what they wanted most of all was for us to tell them until they got old enough to figure it out. I think we'd have been better off with *Mr.* Spock than Dr. Spock."

"But we have tools to—"

"Too late. Use your tools to build the best kind of fort you can. This is the Big Slide, kid. Divine decadence. This is the end of the world we knew. The barbarians aren't at the gates. We're the barbarians."

"Shit, you're pretty smug."

"I can afford to be. I didn't have kids. But if I had, I'm pretty sure I wouldn't let them run my life. And that selfish motive might just give them a little something they could count on in their confusing world. Here's one human being who knows where he'll draw the line."

"Like old Dean Batten?"

I thought about that for a moment. I wanted to be honest and not glib. "Yeah, like Dean Batten. I was on the verge of getting his point. I think that if he'd taken me into the towel locker and punched my guts loose maybe two more times I'd have heard it loud and clear. I might have avoided a lot of what happened later."

"He was a sadist."

"That's a crock. That's one of those stupid labels used

by parents who'd rather have their kids grow up animals than have anybody accuse them of not being progressive. The same people who have neurotic, spoiled pets. Sure, a few of those guys were sadists, but I think Batten was a guy trying to do a tough job in the only way he knew how. He was dealing with kids like me and Happy who were nearly as big as he was but who didn't have any of the fear of consequences that he'd learned, the kind of fear that keeps a lot of people out of trouble. We were the first generation to have our rebellion reinforced by the radio. His was the first generation to have its authority undermined by permissive theories about how to treat children. The combination of those two influences was what tore it all loose. The kids learned to say 'fuck you' and the schools and parents learned to say 'I wonder what they're trying to tell us'."

"But he hit you with his fists."

"We both swung at him. We deserved it. He tried to paddle us, but we couldn't let him do that. He did what he needed to do, what our fathers should have done more often. And we called him a sadist. If you remember, that was how we recruited our parents into getting him off our cases. We fixed him so he'd never punch me and Happy again. It was a triumph for humane and rational values. It was a con. It turned me and Happy loose."

"Are you saying that if Batten had had his way . . . ?"

"I don't know for sure, but I do remember clearly that mostly what we were at that age was willful. Willful without purpose, testing ourselves everywhere, on everybody. Testosterone. It was hard to find anybody who'd stand up to us. Most kids don't push that hard. But we did. Batten was the only one we found who'd push back. Him and a cop named Funderburk who eventually caught the same kind of flak for 'brutalizing' us. I remember a kind of thrill in discovering that Batten wouldn't roll over, a sense of wonder and pleasure that he would go to the *trouble* of punching me out. I liked him. I hated what we did to him. He didn't lose his job, but what happened was worse. We turned him into a modern educator."

"But Happy learned violence from his father. It ruined him. Gary says it starts the cycle, the kids do the same to their kids."

I wasn't sure of myself. "Happy's dad beat his *mother*. He was *drunk*. He was never there when *Happy* needed somebody to stand up to him, or for him. It isn't the same thing. I'm not saying hitting's the only solution. It's a terrible responsibility to take on. And it's quite possible I'm full of crap and Gary's right, but I can only tell you what feels true to me. Does Jennifer pay any attention to Gary?"

Sarah didn't answer. She lit a cigarette with shaking fingers. Her face was very tight and a little gray.

"I'm sorry," I said. "I was careless about your feelings."

We let some time go by. Jean-Pierre removed some dishes and filled her glass again. A gust of wind blew against the board that covered the front window. Jean-Pierre had lowered the aluminum awning and tied it down. There was rain in the wind again, and we heard it racketing against the metal. If the storm came ashore, the awning would peel away like a pop top.

"I'm really pretty ticked at you," she said finally. "I think that if you're so damn smart, you'd better be prepared to tell me what the solution is."

"I'm not sure there *is* one for the Big Slide. Historical inevitability. You could read Epictetus, Boethius. It's time for the consolation of philosophy."

"You're really a worse smart-ass than you were," she said, although I thought her mood was improving.

Jean-Pierre came with coffee. "There's an old Wobbly slogan," I said. "'Rebuild the new world within the shell of the old.' Something like that."

Jean-Pierre stood up after pouring, the coffeepot held like some ceremonial relic. "Lorca is more romantic," he said, smiling. "'Let the wedding go on within the war.'"

Sarah smiled then and Jean-Pierre made a subtle but classy exit with a fifty I had slipped him.

"I saw that," Sarah said. "I pay expenses."

"Not when I ruin your evening. Besides, your credit card would spoil the whole thing for Jean-Pierre, who seems to have the highest sort of romantic hopes for us."

"You wish," Sarah said, in a schoolgirl voice.

"How's Beth?"

"Took you long enough to get to that. She says she'd love to see you, that she won't have an affair with you, and that you're not to have one with me, either."

"I guess that covers twenty years. The most important thing for both of you is still to keep me and Happy from getting the only thing we really wanted."

We both laughed. "Do you remember how hard we worked for it?" I asked. "We even pointed out the truth to you both—that your reputations were automatically compromised by virtue, you should pardon the expression, of going out with us. What difference could it make to keep struggling with us over your virginity?"

"You told Beth I was giving it to Happy and lying to her. He told me the same thing about you and Beth. Nobody's ever worked harder for anything. But we were determined not to give it up to a couple of hard cases like you two. Maybe if we'd seen signs of reform."

"That's why we couldn't reform. We were too sexually frustrated to join mainstream society. It's all your fault that we turned out so bad. And then you gave it to the first two nice boys who came along after us. Guys you didn't even like that much. Didn't you?"

"Yes. We both did. I guess it didn't make any sense. They seemed safe. We'd practically grown up saying no to you two. When you were gone, it didn't seem so important. Or maybe it was just timing."

"Tell her hello."

"She wants to know what we find on our quest, too."

"We may not find anything, but it has to start in St. Pete, and, weather permitting, I'll start tomorrow."

We said goodnight to Jean-Pierre and drove around the key before going home. "If it stayed like this I'd buy a house here," I said.

"If it stayed like this you could afford one."

The little red Audi was gone. Sarah climbed the stairs like a fireman in a four-alarmer and was reading the note when I got there, holding Jennifer's food in a styrofoam container.

"Damn her," she said, handing it to me. "She must have had a duplicate key made."

"Dear Mom," Jennifer had written. "I've gone to Orlando, to Cissy's. You know I'll be safe and don't worry about me. You and Randy take care and be good. See you after the storm. Love, Jenny."

Sarah made a drink and lit a cigarette. We sat for a while in the living room. "You quit drinking," she said, her voice a little shaky with anger and fear. "You quit drugs. You quit smoking. How do you handle this stupid life? Does all that righteousness give you strength?"

"No," I said. "I just wore it out. I couldn't do it any more, and I couldn't die. This is what I ended up with."

We listened to the wind. "Tell me *something*," she said finally. "I'm paying your expenses."

"We've been philosophical all night. That hasn't helped."

"Don't spare me. What's the secret, gumshoe? What's the bird's-eye lowdown on this caper?"

"We all die," I said, surprising myself.

She almost laughed. "Thank you. *Now* I feel better."

"I didn't mean to say that."

"Now that you have, pray continue."

"Or, as a wise philosopher friend of mine used to say,

if you're going to fuck the dog, you might as well stick it in all the way."

"How charming." She made a face, rolling her eyes like a teenager. She was feeling better.

"You should feel better," I said. "It's very liberating."

"Everybody knows we die. What are you talking about?"

"Everybody pays it lip service, like God. Yeah, I know nobody lives forever. Yeah, I believe in God. But the truth of it didn't really hit me until a couple of years ago. Came out of nowhere. It's really *true*. Whatever I am, I will not last forever. Maybe I have a few years left before I find out what it's like not to exist anymore. It's a little spooky at first, I'll admit, but it gets better. It puts everything in a different light. It's the deepest kind of mystery, the only important riddle. I'd seen so many people die. I'd come so close to dying. But it just didn't register. Maybe you have to be a certain age."

"Or have a friend who'll bring you the wonderful message."

"Shucks," I said, "I wouldn't do this for my ordinary clients."

She took a long pull on her drink and finished her cigarette. She ground it into the ashtray and watched until no more smoke came from it. "You mean you don't have to struggle quite so hard to hold it all together?"

"Yeah. And it all seems more interesting, more forgivable, downright poignant. Maybe even precious."

"I'll have to think about that. I'm going to need a sleeping pill tonight. You want one?"

"I guess not."

"Good. You'll keep us safe."

"Sure."

She gave my hand a squeeze and left me. I heard her bedroom door close. I had wanted to tell her how peaceful I felt, how secure. I didn't understand it myself. In the guest room I crawled under the sheets and listened to the wind circle and growl like some friendly dog guarding us. I fell asleep.

Sarah woke me later when she crawled into bed. "No cute stuff," she said, and turned her back to me. "Just hold me."

Five

Sarah left my bed before daybreak, or what would have been daybreak. I slept a little longer, then got up and let her fix us some bagels and hot tea. A different excited TV weatherman told us that there had been no change in the storm's location or strength. The Sunshine Skyway was closed because of the high winds. Bridge traffic should be very careful. Several vans and trucks had been blown over, though none had yet gone into the bay. Motorists without important business should stay at home. Those who had taken shelter inland should remain there. Do not, repeat, not, grow complacent. "Fat chance of that," Sarah said to the TV screen.

I stowed all my gear in the Eagle again, putting the other pistols in my suitcase and the Colt in the glove compartment. Sarah wrote me a check to cover expenses for a while and asked me to call her that night if I decided not to return to Sarasota. I said I'd call her either way and we hugged each other good-bye, neither of us mentioning the way we'd slept. I took the back way around the bay to Tampa and over I-275 to St. Pete, listening to a folk show on WMNF, that left-of-the-dial station, and several songs recorded together by Si Kahn and John McCutcheon, two Carolina folkies whose work I knew. They were singing about how bad things are and about a New Age. Like the Wobblies, they wanted to build a new world inside the shell of the old. As Sarah might say, fat chance.

I drove around St. Pete for a while, ambushed by childhood memories. The Pheil Theater was gone, where Happy and I had watched *Blackboard Jungle* when we were still too young to act it out. I remembered how it felt when we heard Bill Haley and the Comets kick into "Rock Around the Clock." Something new, something electric. Something made us shiver. Something started then. We were just barely old enough to take the bus downtown alone, but we knew we wanted to be part of that new thing, wanted to be gritty, greasy, exotic, dangerous, bad. Ike was playing golf. Kennedy was a senator. Before Cuba, Berlin, Dallas. What did we know about bad? I remember standing outside the theater afterward, watching the ordinary cars go by, wondering how we could bring that kind of excitement to our dull lives. We found it; it found us.

The Florida Theater was gone, too. We'd stood in a line that reached twice around the block to see Elvis. Liggett's Drugs was closed, and even if it weren't, the magazines would now be wrapped in cellophane, the cherry cokes pre-mixed in Atlanta, and Crazy Willy probably on Thorazine. My dad's men's wear store was now a thrift shop run by an outfit I'd never heard of. The Haddads's millinery shop (then called Mazie's) had become a gentrified fern café. People (mainly kids) watch movies these days in shopping malls, in "multi-cinema" units built like restroom stalls where the soundtracks leak together and everybody talks during the shows. I'm sure we talked during the movies, too, but they showed matinees for kids on Saturdays and kept us out of the adults' hair.

Old "Rot" Wise had brought *Blackboard Jungle* back to his Sun Art Theater about once a month until the Summer of Love came along and made it unfashionable. Later Rot showed *Easy Rider*, alternating with nudist camp movies, burlesque tease loops, and promos for art films that never arrived. Now it was hard core, I guessed. Rot was always in the vanguard. One of the punks from *Blackboard Jungle* grew up to wear a dress in *M*A*S*H* and now does commercials for a candy bar on TV. This was all O.K. by me. I don't expect time to stand still. I hadn't even planned to try to go home again.

I found a parking space right outside the St. Petersburg *Times*. I took the elevator to the right floor, located the morgue desk and cleared my throat, wondering idly what approach, if one was necessary, to use. It's always best to have your story cold when you're pretending to be someone you aren't, but most papers are pretty free with their files, and besides, there was a hurricane offshore.

The girl who came around the partition made it very difficult to think. I had a little trouble talking at first. I stood there staring for a while, like Crazy Willy wandered in from the street. She was olive on pink, a kind of overlay of complexions, as if someone in makeup had begun to turn a beautiful, freckled Irish girl into a Polynesian maiden and stopped to admire the wonderful accident. She had long, glossy, dark-brown hair in a single braid to her waist. She was tall, slender and yet somehow voluptuous, too, and graceful as a palm tree. I guessed her to be in her late twenties. She had what the fashion poofs call bone structure, a small, pert, European nose and almond-shaped light-brown eyes. She was a gorgeous mongrel.

But she wasn't perfect. Lucky for me. She was blinking in a way that suggested new contacts and a certain vanity about her old spectacles. She was dressed in the thrift-shop style which suggested an Eckerd College student or someone else who really cared about the important things. She had ink under her nails.

"I'm looking for a friend," I said.

"The advertising department is on the first floor," she said, smiling.

"We're meeting cute," I said, "like in the movies."

"I hope you're not offended," she said. "It's just something I always wanted to do. Let's start again."

"Sure. I'm looking for an old friend and your files have several stories about him which might give me a lead. I was hoping you could Xerox them for me. I'll pay for copies, of course."

"What's the friend's name?"

"Fox. Edward Allen Fox."

"And if I give you everything we have on him will you not report my impertinence to my superiors?"

"I used to know a lot of people here," I said. "I doubt that you have any superiors."

She acknowledged the compliment with a slight curtsy and disappeared. There was a fresh paper on the counter and I scanned it as I waited. The front page was all storm, the second mostly more weather. On page three was a story about the slaughter of two girls camped in South Carolina. I read it closely, felt the old familiar crawl, and knew where my roadside acquaintance had gone. I went over to the coin-operated machine and made a copy—I don't know why. The girl came back with a file and saw what I'd copied. Then she looked at what she was carrying. She put on a new face, less playful and more flattering and maybe a little hungry, like a cat near your bait bucket. "This is quite a package," she said. "It might take a while. Would you like to see what I've got so far? A lot of this was already copied."

I said yes and thank you.

"I saw you reading about the campground creep. You don't know him, too, do you?"

I said no. She seemed to be trying to make a connection that I knew didn't exist.

"Are you with the police?" she asked.

"No," I said.

"The paper has pretty strict rules about handing out a whole file like this. Obviously, I'm breaking them. My supervisor stayed home and the storm has made a certain amount of latitude possible, but don't tell anybody where you got it." I thanked her again and she handed me a folder full of Xerox copies of news clips on Edward Allen "Happy" Fox. She showed me a desk in an empty office where I could look them over. I watched her walk away, her braid in lovely counterbalance to her hips. She looked back over her shoulder and caught me at it.

Six

I wished I could look at her and not Happy's file. Now that I was here I had little stomach for it. But this was how I would find him, if I could find him. This might also be a painful way of finding a part of myself I'd hoped to lose.

I didn't know he'd been married. There was the traditional announcement. There had been a double-ring ceremony at a Lutheran church, a reception at the home of somebody I didn't know, but whose address I noted, no honeymoon plans but a place of residence for the new couple, which I also noted. The best man was Peter Pollard. The ushers were Aldo Rizzo and Elton Huddle.

I had what you need if you're going to find somebody—the names of friends. Even if somebody is trying to hide—and I still had no reason to believe Happy was the least bit bashful—most of us tell somebody our story. The need to tell our story is not far behind the needs for food and sex. Very few individuals have what it takes to stay disappeared: the ability to keep moving and never, ever, tell anyone who you are. Not your old name, not any name with any association with yours, not anything about your real past, or anything about your true interests.

Most people find a friend, a mate, a new town, and try

to stop running. If they work they may use a different name and apply for social security, using their true birthdate. Sometimes they use their real social security number. If they do get themselves involved with paper—steady job, driver's license, car registration, marriage or divorce, social security, pension and entitlements—you can often find them through a paper chase—or a computer version of one. Coffey will sometimes help me with that. He's a homicide detective sergeant in Atlanta. We helped each other out once and may again.

The only way to avoid paper is to do temporary work or have money and never give a name unless you have to, and then never one remotely like yours and never the same one twice. You get an unknown vehicle and steal appropriate plates for whatever state you're in and don't keep them long. You drive carefully and don't talk to anyone and never do what you're known to like to do, or even let anyone know you're alive, no matter how anonymously, and never break the law so you're stopped and questioned. I hoped Happy wasn't trying to stay lost—for his sake more than mine—or trying too hard to lose his old friends.

The next clip was a curious example of the headline writer's art: YOUTH CHARGED IN NOSE PUNCHING. It was another road hassle, this time with two hog-riders in their twenties. There was no way to figure what put Happy onto two bikers. They insulted him; he insulted them; life was an insult to all concerned and it felt good to bash somebody for it. It read as if Happy had done most of the bashing. He had "leaped from his vehicle," in the unlikely words of Mr. Eugene Worthy, one of the bikers, "and assaulted us." Happy was even charged with damage to the two Harleys. He spent the night in jail where he was charged with assaulting another prisoner, who was taken to the hospital for treatment.

Perhaps the greatest mystery of Happy Fox had always

been his uncanny ability to punch people's noses with such almost universal results. I'd grown up with him, and it was still hard to understand. I've heard that if you want to learn strength, carry a calf every day until it is fully grown. And if you want to learn to jump, begin jumping a sapling and jump it every day until it is too high to jump. There was something like the psychological equivalent of that with me and Happy. I had known him too long to fear him.

We boxed a lot, especially in the long summers. We'd turn on the old AM, make a pitcher of iced tea, open his Florida room windows so we could hear the music, and chase each other around a ring we had marked with chalk on the heat-browned, parched, St. Augustine grass of his tiny lawn. On Saturdays, after we were older, we would join Gus at the Police Athletic League ring on Madeira Beach. He would set the matches and Happy and I, Junior, Aldo, Petey, and any other semi-serious pugilists and punks would fight until we got thirsty and broke for beer.

That was how I learned to carry the calf, jump the sapling. I knew Happy was good, but most of us were good, too, and I can still move my hands. What Happy seemed to have on the street was beyond skill, beyond mere physical gifts. His responses to challenges from outsiders were so instantaneous and committed that in many cases by the time I was committed he was finished with his man and jumping someone else. He had learned to bypass the reflections that give most of us pause, learned to do what obviously needed to be done in the shortest possible time without crippling self-examination, doubt, without a fraction of a second's hesitation. It seemed very simple for him. If you crossed a line he had drawn in his head, he was your enemy, quicker than thought and utterly ferocious until the exact moment that he knew you were finished.

Granted, he had physical gifts. I've seen him leave his feet to reach a bigger opponent and hit him three times before landing. The accuracy of his punches was amazing, considering his limited size and reach. But many of us were fast, and some of us were stronger, and I outreached him every day of our lives, and we couldn't do that. I'm a head taller and in our punk days probably had at least fifteen pounds on him, and I wish I had a trophy for every time a guy refused to fight Happy and jumped me instead.

Most of us have to think about it a little, and that slows us down. If you're asking yourself any of the obvious questions that most people ask themselves about the risk of physical violence, you're already behind. Sure, we've all known people who didn't hesitate because they were stupid, but Happy was far from stupid. He was one of the few bright individuals I'd known who had learned that samurai art of the automatic and fully committed physical response to a threat. It was that aspect of the SEAL mission which drew me, and it was what I'd looked for in karate. I'd found a few men who seemed able to do it, but I had never quite learned to do it reliably, in every instance, myself. Maybe nobody could do that in our modern world. Not every time. Not and stay out of jail. In feudal Japan it was an easier distinction to make, easier to draw the line at which a certain behavior called for a certain response.

And of course the line in Happy's head was more and more distorted. His definition of threat and challenge had turned into a kind of furious paranoia that included everyone he might conceivably "nose-punch." I still didn't understand it. There was a moment somewhere in the time spanned by these clips when Happy turned away from his good options and plunged into a life that could only have led him to jail. Had it come when he decided not to go to college? I knew he'd been able to go to the local junior college. I was there and I'd encouraged him to come along. He'd dropped by a few times, sat around the tables in the student union and heard our college-boy fraternity-party lies. He could have made the transition; I did.

I found a clip about an accident and remembered that I'd heard something about it. It would have been about the same time—our freshman year of college. Local youths had driven off the seawall of one of the newer landfills at a high rate of speed. They were apparently drag-racing with another vehicle which stopped short of the seawall and then left the scene. They were all drunk. The driver, Edward Allen Fox, had sustained serious injuries to his head. Also listed were Elton Huddle, Peter Pollard, and Aldo Rizzo.

Why hadn't I remembered the accident more clearly? There were several follow-up stories about Happy's long and uncertain recovery. Had I gone to see him? What was I doing? I was reading books and drinking from kegs and trying to bump in the night as many college girls as I could. I was smoking dope and listening to the first of a newer kind of rock and roll and discovering jazz and learning disdain already for my silly college friends. If I had outgrown beer parties in that short year, how much farther must I have felt from Happy and the "boys," still cruising and drinking and bashing other greasers? Had I gone to see him in the hospital? There was a vague memory, one of those you think might be the product of guilt and wishful thinking.

Why were we so fascinated with fistfighting? Man is the only animal to do it. One of the great apes might try to smash you with a bottom fist, or a bear might slap you, or a kangaroo wave his paws at your face. But only man has made a science of striking his fellow man, a "sweet" science of the physics of the clenched fist and the ballistics of the knuckle against a variety of human surfaces, a study which thrived in ancient Greece and China and seemed to have begun in prehistory. Is it an accident—like the thorn one of Darwin's finches learned to use as a tool—or is it as natural as it looked when a man like Happy did it? Was he a freak of pugilistic adaptation to a world which had decided later to change the rules?

The beautiful morgue girl brought me the rest of the clips and asked if she could stay and read with me. I was too absorbed to consider it and she just sat down. I took a few minutes to organize all the clippings chronologically and handed her the ones I'd finished. Many of them were the afternoon paper's version of the same events. Some of it went way back and was relatively innocent, like a little clip about a birthday party Happy's mother threw for him and his friends on his twelfth birthday. I was there.

But most of it got worse. Judge Hess had tried him on the several counts related to the assault on the lawyer. He had decided to make an example of him and combined the local maximum on every count to make the longest city-jail sentence anyone had ever been given in that jurisdiction. There was Happy's mugshot, his face swollen with sullen rage. Then he had assaulted other prisoners, been caught with an overdose of barbiturates which he told the judge he planned to take, and tried to hang himself with a rolled up sheet. He had apparently written numerous letters to the judge, demanding most of the considerations that it occurs to jailhouse lawyers to demand. Officer George Funderburk, a man who seemed to specialize in arresting Happy, was quoted as saying that Edward Fox hadn't "a single redeeming quality."

Then there was a long period of silence, a gap of some eight months before the next notice of Happy Fox. In a controversial decision, the judge had released him, conditional on his agreement to leave the state and rehabilitate himself under the supervision of his sister in California. No address was given, nor was his sister's name. The reporter had been asked for his discretion, I suspected. The reporter might still know, but I had better leads than that. The judge was one, too. Apparently they carried on a correspondence that might have continued.

The judge explained his decision in several newspaper interviews. He felt, based on his own experience with Fox and Mrs. Fox's assurances, that Happy could be rehabilitated and would not profit from any further imprisonment. He was apparently taking some heat, but he stuck by it and Happy got onto a plane.

There was a gap of almost three years before the last of the Happy Fox file. It was a major feature story in the morning paper and an even larger one in the afternoon *Independent* about Happy's return to preach the Lord's truth, as he had discovered it, to those in the grip of drugs and street crime. He'd gone to all the dingy and embarrassing places with his ministry. This was later in the seventies. The first headline was BAD BOY RETURNS WITH LORD'S FIGHT. The second read PUNK TO JESUS FREAK. There was a picture of Happy with jeans and boots, long hair and granny glasses. There was his testimony:

"I'd rather have Jesus than the world," Happy told a reporter. "My old friends hate me now. They think I burned out on acid. I came back to show them I hadn't, but they don't want to hear it. I didn't want to hear it either. It took my total defeat before I could open my eyes to Christ, open my ears to his voice."

Happy's troubles had continued in California. Although he hadn't any problems with the law and avoided fights, he was drinking a lot and using the whole range of available drugs. "I'd met a guy on the beach one night when I was really torn up. He tried to tell me about Jesus. I walked away from him but something stuck in my mind. I gave a girl a ride one day and found myself asking her if she believed in God. She said she had been a Christian and wanted to find God again. A week later we were married. My first wife had divorced me while I was in jail. But we couldn't seem to get free of drugs. It was so hard to stop. I prayed for help.

"I'm not sure whether it was an audible voice or whether I heard it in my heart. I was lying in bed late one night, miserable. I had this sudden understanding. Something was floating in the room. I was very afraid. I couldn't raise my head. I got on my knees and said, 'Jesus, I give up.' Now I have a reason to live. I carry God's message to other people."

The article described Happy's efforts to help the drug kids on Clearwater Beach, his visits to local missions, his rejection by old friends. "I've learned to turn the other cheek," he said. He had apparently lived in St. Petersburg for several months, pamphleteering and preaching. His second wife was with him, pregnant, and his young son, whose name, the paper said, was Christian. An address was given. I wrote it down.

I passed the last story to the morgue girl. She read it with apparent fascination. I watched her. It was a lot more fun than thinking about Happy. She looked up and said: "I'm Leila Sweeting. This is a fascinating story." She held out her hand and I took it. It was warm and a little wet and it felt good. I told her my name and we kept on holding hands until we both looked down and laughed and let go. "I'm a writer," she said. "I'm looking for a great feature story that I can use to show what I can do, something I can use to get a better job."

"Here?"

"Better, if I can. They keep stalling me here. I didn't major in journalism, for chrissake. I didn't go to the University of Florida."

"You think this is a good story?"

"A great magazine story, especially if you find him, especially if it adds up. May I tag along, so to speak?"

"I don't think he's here anymore. There'd be a follow-up story, or I'd have heard somehow if he were still here. I think this is going to take me out west, or someplace else, and it may still not be a story. Maybe I won't find him"

"Maybe you're going to write it. I didn't—"

"No, writing's too hard. That's why I do this kind of work."

"You mean you're *hired* to do this?" I told her the circumstances of my employment. I showed her the wallet-sized, photo I.D. copy of my North Carolina P.I. license and she read my whole name aloud: "Randall Gatsby Sierra?"

"My dad was a big fan of Scott Fitzgerald."

She hesitated, not wanting to seem too eager. She couldn't find another way and said: "I've got two weeks' vacation time coming. This is a good time to take it."

I hesitated, not wanting to be so eager, knowing all the bad turns a deal like this could take, knowing the odds against a sane girl wanting to go along on a ride like this. "You don't know me. You could be in for a lot of trouble. I could be Ted Bundy or something. Maybe I stole my ID."

"I know," she said. "That's why I thought I'd invite you for supper tonight, see if maybe we spook each other. Then we could call it off."

"We can call it off any time."

"I understand. Let's just try it."

"What time tonight?"

"Around six. I get off at five, so come earlier if you're finished. If we have power I'll cook you something nice. If not, we'll eat tuna sandwiches and raw veggies by the light of a hurricane lamp."

She gave me the address and I thanked her.

"I have a couch if you need it," she said. "Don't misunderstand me."

"Thank you."

"I'm not finished helping you yet," she said. "I think I know where you can find Petey Pollard."

Seven

Leila told me that a guy named Peter Pollard had hung out around Eckerd College for several years. The physical description seemed to fit, but the rest didn't. "He was a sweet guy, really. Older than most of us. He lived nearby, and he may still live there. I went to a party there one time. I think he was involved in trying to open a couple folk clubs on the south side of town, and a kind of student bar and restaurant. None of those things last. I know he took courses in the art department and learned to make jewelry. I think that's mainly what he does now."

I shook my head.

"People change," she said, taking my hand again and leading me out to another office where there was a phone book and a city directory. "Let's see."

"O.K.," I said, "but first I check a couple of obvious leads." I looked for Fox in the phone book. The only one was the Foxes' Den, a topless bar on US 19 up near Piney Park. I checked the cross-referenced city directory for Fox. Sometimes you'll get a listing there even if the phone book doesn't pay off. Nothing. I looked under the address last given for Happy and his evangelical little brood. Someone else was living there. I went back to the phone book and found Judge Hess. I called him at home and his wife said he was doing some last-minute work at the courthouse and could he call me back. I said I'd call again and tried him at the courthouse. Nobody could find him, though he'd been there. Maybe he was on his way home.

There was a Peter Pollard listed, not far from where Eckerd made a little oasis between the crass commercial strip leading to the Skyway and the black ghetto, which even before I left had expanded to include most of the south side. Eckerd had changed over the years, but it had always been a refuge for some of the nicest freaks in this part of the state. Eckerd students had lived for years in the cheap housing left behind by fleeing whites, in more or less comfortable proximity to their black and poor white neighbors and to some of the Eastern European refugees who had stayed behind. I noted the address and number.

"Call it," she said. "I bet it's the same guy."

"You didn't know him," I said, but I dialed.

A mellow-hip voice answered. You've heard it. I'm not sure what it is certain people do to get that quality, but this guy had it. It means I'm a gentle fellow, in tune with nature. It means women will be safe with me. It means I have principles and yet I'm tolerant, maybe even of you. It means I have an enormous record collection, most of it people you never heard of. It means plants and grass to smoke and wind chimes and herbal tea. I don't have a thing in the world against this kind of guy except that he makes me feel like a Visigoth with blood on his hands and shit on his shoes. And Petey Pollard is never going to talk like this.

"Is this the Peter Pollard who went to Boca Ciega High?" I asked. "Did you used to be a friend of Happy Fox?"

"Yes, I did," he said. "Who is this?"

I told him who I was while Leila grinned and poked me

in the ribs. He seemed as glad to hear from me as a mellow-hip guy will allow himself to get and made me promise to come by and see him. He asked me if I'd heard from Happy. I said not since he was in St. Pete, but I was looking for him. Had he heard anything? He said he had gotten an envelope full of religious pamphlets and had even written Happy a letter, but he wasn't sure he still had any of them around. I asked him where the envelope came from and he said somewhere in California. He couldn't remember exactly where. I asked him to look for the pamphlets. "One thing I remember," he said, "because it seemed strange. There were various addresses on the different pamphlets of the people who printed them. Most of them seemed to be from Ohio. Then there was a rubber stamp on every pamphlet with Happy's group's name and address in California. It looked like he bought the pamphlets he liked from wherever he could find them, then just stamped them as his own."

"What was his group's name?"

"Christian Soldiers. I remember that. It suited him. But the literature didn't, really. I think I wrote him that he'd be more persuasive if he wrote about his personal experience instead of just mailing tracts. I think I tried to explain that most people are turned off by stuff that looks like that. I think he just sent me some more tracts."

"What did they look like?"

"You know the kind of stuff. Drugs are the devil's tool. Rock and roll is Satan's voice. Like that."

I told Petey I hoped he could find some of them and he said he'd look. I promised to drive over soon.

"Take care," he said. "There's a hurricane offshore."

I tried Judge Hess again and he answered, out of breath. "Hold on," he said. "I just ran in. There's a power line down on our street."

I waited for him. When he'd caught his breath I told him what I was looking for. It was silly, since I was the one who had to do the talking, but people get silly during a storm, like kids or kittens in the charged air.

"California," he said. "I'm sure of that."

He sounded like a decent man. Happy had been very lucky to get him. "Can you tell me where?"

"If I could get at my files, I could. If I can get in tomorrow I'll try to find his letters. I know I kept them at the courthouse."

"Did you keep any of the pamphlets?"

"No, I'm afraid not. I was glad to see him changed, but they weren't my cup of tea."

"A little heavy handed?"

"A good deal so."

"I wonder if you could tell me something, your honor," I said. "I grew up with him. We were very close. Another of his old friends has asked me to find him. We want to be sure he's all right. What was it persuaded you to let him out early?"

"The newspapers already asked me this."

"I'm not a reporter. I'm a friend. Off the record. His mother was a good woman."

"Yes, it was partly his mother, and partly his sister in California, a very fine young woman who came with her husband and pleaded his case. She promised to give him a place to make a new start."

"Officer Funderburk said he hadn't a redeeming quality. It was in one of the clips I read today. Is that how he seemed to you?"

"I don't like to believe there are many people like that. There was something in his letters, something between the lines."

"So you were pretty sure he was no threat to society?"

"No," he answered. I think storms promote honesty, too. "I can't say that. All judges are wrong some of the time. We live with the possibility that we'll ruin a good man or set another Ted Bundy free."

"Do you remember his sister's married name or where she lived?"

"No, I'm afraid not, but it will be in the files. Call me here tomorrow after noon. If I can get in or if I can reach my secretary and she can get in, I'll have it for you."

"Thank you, your honor."

"I just hope I can get to it."

"I mean thanks for Happy."

"I'm glad it helped. Please let me know how he's doing, when you find him."

Petey's place was farther south and my route took me close enough to the old neighborhood so that I turned the wheel at Fifth Avenue—something in me resisting strongly anything so obvious—and went home again.

My old house looked great. It was, if anything, in better shape than when we lived there. A black man carried an armful of cabbage palm fronds toward the garage where my old man had puttered around his boats and outboards and lawnmowers. Two small children, a boy and a girl, watched the black father struggle. He'd probably been told by one of those nervous TV weathermen that a missile like that could be driven right through a wall or a human skull by the force of a hurricane. The house next door was not so well tended. A rusted old Ford GT rested on concrete blocks and the yard was overrun by sandspurs. Nobody was worrying about the dead fronds hanging from its palms.

I drove slowly down Fourth toward where Happy used to live. The block had a Caribbean quality now—brighter colors and more differences among the houses than in the all-white days in which seventy percent of the homes built here had either coral or aquamarine trim and either the plaster palm tree or marlin near the front door.

Smell is the sense that tugs my memory backward.

From somewhere deep inside my life came the smell of mud along the curbs, sharp and funky, stinging the nostrils in the harsh, summer sun. A kid walks. He gets closer to those smells. Part of him remembers. The gutters today were washed with hurricane rain and the air was cool for September, but there it was anyway, as insistent and real as the storm around me. For a moment I remembered how it felt to be a kid in a hurry with nothing to do, excited and bored, his whole life before him, still too young to worry. I drove up the alley to Happy's old place, the way I'd come long ago. But the alley was blocked by a fallen punk tree, so I backed up and parked and did it on foot, like the old days.

I heard something with a rap beat from the house across the alley. (If we have to fill another ark, somebody will try to bring a jam box aboard.) Happy's house was quiet. I wondered if it might be empty. I never saw an obit for his mom, or his dad, for that matter. My parents were both gone, but there was no reason why his had to be. They weren't listed in the phone book, but they may have stopped wanting phone calls about their son. Or the solicitation vultures may have driven them, like many other phone-victimized elderly, to the ranks of the unlisted. The patch where we used to fight between Happy's and the next house beyond was still worn and the St. Augustine grass still brown around it—even puddled as it was with rain. I came up in back to knock on the screen enclosure door.

It seemed too small. Everything from your youth seems too small if you do go home again. This shabby yard couldn't have been the training field for two such gladiators. This tiny-frame asphalt-shingled house couldn't have been the forum for such brilliant and far-reaching conversations as we had. How could two such dangerous characters have forged the steel of their will in this tacky, flimsy little screen enclosure? I knocked, waited, then knocked more loudly and said yoo-hoo, a phrase which hadn't passed my lips in some time. Who could fear a man who said yoo-hoo?

I looked around the yard as if to say, see, I'm doing no harm. Of course it's exactly what the collection boys and process servers and other weasels do, although usually they try the front door first. I saw a blind bent up in the Florida room next door and walked over to knock there. The blind went down. Nobody answered at first. I said yoo-hoo again.

"Vat you vant?" somebody said from the blinded porch.

"I'm looking for Mr. Fox, who used to live next door. May I talk with you?"

"Da fader?" the voice said.

I didn't know what that meant at first, but suddenly I knew who this man was. Mr. Rankaitis, whom we called, of course, Mr. Bronchitis, had complained about our radio, our boxing, our treatment of the grass—though it was not on his yard. He had been a persistent if tolerable curmudgeonly voice through our youth. Mrs. Fox had tried to mollify him and we had learned mostly to ignore him. He was still there. He had fled Lithuania, only to spend most of his life in the free world huddled behind Venetian blinds in a sun-bleached Florida ghetto.

"Not the father, Mr. Rankaitis," I said. "Happy. I'm Randy Sierra. I know you. I used to be Happy's friend."

There was a pause. "Da fader dead," he said. "Moder die too, two years."

"Who lives there now, Mr. Rankaitis?"

"Black woman. Good woman. Daughter good too. They not home. I call police."

"I won't bother their house."

"Dese other people not good," he said. "Terrible place to live."

"I'm looking for Happy, Mr. Rankaitis."

Another pause. "Appy good boy," he said finally, his voice rising challengingly. "People no treat people dis way when Appy live here. He punch dey face."

"Did Mrs. Fox say where Happy was?"

"You one of those bad boys fight here, hurt de grass?"

"Yes." Mr. Rankaitis seemed to have forgotten the virtues of our pugilism, but I didn't feel like lying.

"You good boys," he said, giving in to relativity. Then he said: "Appy live San Louis."

I thanked him and walked back down the alley to my car. I was tired of standing in people's yards, tired of looking at my cheap little childhood, tired of getting rained on and feeling sorry for Mr. Rankaitis. St. Louis my ass. I'd never seen more than his shadow against the blinds. Maybe, after all these years, that's all there was left.

Eight

Petey's house was surrounded by a large, wooden fence, unpainted and, to my surprise, also untouched by graffiti. I wouldn't have expected a white man to be able to live behind a tall fence in a black neighborhood without some visible marks of conflict, but then I'd been up in the mountains for a while and didn't know what new kinds of deals had been made. Most of the other houses seemed well tended. Maybe Petey was chairman of the Neighborhood Action Committee. He'd already surprised me.

The gate wasn't locked and I walked up to the door to knock. The small house had been covered with natural wood shingles, and the door and other trim were painted a friendly, Scandinavian-looking shade of blue. A window was open and I heard him call: "Randy, come in."

We met just inside—a fat, white, short-haired dog first and then Petey, who gave me one of those '70s power handshakes without a moment of self-consciousness and then opened his arms for what was for both of us an awkward Human Potential Movement hug. It wasn't easy, trying to pick appropriate signals from the years which had separated us. The last time we'd met, the closest we'd have come to affection would have been to hand a beer. Beer-tossing came later, in TV commercials, where visual possibilities of lifestyles were exploited and tubesteaks threw beer cans all over the landscape. We knew, in the old days, that if you threw beer around it got foamy and exploded when you opened it and you couldn't drink much of it. Anybody who threw a beer was a dork.

Seeing that Petey was older reminded me that I was older. Mirrors are much kinder and more gradual than old friends you haven't seen in a while. Petey said "Come" and I followed him through a hallway into what was his studio. The dog was satisfied and stayed behind. There was a very well-made wooden display case with a glass cover. "My work," he said. He worked in gold and semi-precious stones—pendants, rings, earrings, brooches, most of them with a climbing-vine motif. There was even a golden cross with vines worked around it. "I'd like to buy that," I said, pointing.

"Thanks for the compliment," he said. "Is it for a girl?"

"No. I'm not sure who it's for. I just like it."

"Maybe Happy's wife will like it," he said in that mellow voice. "I wish I'd done something to help, but I couldn't think of what to do. I was in the Army when he went to jail."

"I didn't know that. You weren't drafted."

"No. I hoped I'd find something."

"You find 'Nam?"

"Yeah. Walking tour, mostly. I had good scores so they let me be a medic."

"Long way from making this nice jewelry."

"Not so long, really. I came back and by then there was a heavy draft and so I helped draft resisters. I met a lot of nice people at Eckerd. I had the GI Bill. I learned how to do this. I tried music, theater, business, but this is what I do best. I heard you were a SEAL."

"I blew out my knee on the last jump at Benning. I'd had most of the fun training, but I wasn't any good to them after that, so I finished my short-time as a journalist on an ASW carrier in the North Atlantic. I'm glad it went that way. I never killed anybody." I was hoping that Petey would accept that lie. I hadn't killed anyone as a SEAL and I didn't want to talk about the others.

Petey didn't exactly reassure me. "I hard some other rumors."

"Well, I worked for the sheriff while I was going to school—over at USF. Then I got pretty weird for a few years. Lots of drugs, drank a lot. Made some ugly friends and had a few ugly jobs. A lot like Happy, but I didn't find God."

"But you got straight."

"Yes. A day at a time and all that."

"So you must have found something."

"I don't know. What I found isn't nearly so clear to me as it seems to him."

"Maybe he's changed, too. Anyway, give him this cross."

"I'll tell him it's from you."

He took it from the case. It was a pleasure to see a man handle the thing he'd discovered he did best. He put it into a little lined case and handed it to me. "It'll be from you, too," he said. "Both of us. No charge. Try not to be such a hard ass."

"I'm a private eye," I said, trying to lighten the conversation. "It's expected. When your partner finds Jesus you're supposed to do something about it."

Petey let me keep it light. I followed him to the kitchen and he made us some tea. "Could you find any of the pamphlets?" I asked.

"I'm sorry," he said.

"Where can I find Aldo and Junior?"

"That's easier. Aldo's married, very lower-middle-class. He runs a shop that makes camper tops for trucks. Makes pretty good money. Spends it taking his family places in a truck with a camper top. He's in the book.

Sorry for the sarcasm."

"I can't resist a little social commentary from time to time myself," I admitted. "Junior?"

Petey sighed. "Junior's still at Dottie's Tavern on the beach. He does some commercial fishing. Had his own boat, but it was too much responsibility. He fishes, then drinks, then fishes, and so on. With the storm out there, you won't have any trouble finding him."

"But Dottie must be dead by now."

"She is. New management. Junior's still not sure he can break them in properly. I went out and had a beer with him about a year ago. It did not lift my spirits, but he said Happy had written him, too."

"I'll try it."

Petey sipped his tea. "I'd go with you," he said. "But a year hasn't been long enough ago. You actually do this for a living?"

"Sarah Diehl hired me for this one. She's paying expenses, anyway. I'm not charging for the time."

"Sarah Diehl," Petey said, in a reverential voice. He might have used the same voice to say Guinevere or Cleopatra or Aphrodite.

"She said she thought you deserved to make it," I told him. "I'll tell her that you did."

"Yeah?" he said, his voice having lost any trace of mellow, his face in a happy high school grin. "She said that? Damn!"

I left him there at the table, smiling back through the years. Sometimes this is not such a bad way to make a living.

Nine

Aldo lived on the north side, in a house like the ones we used to have on the south side, with aquamarine trim and a plaster palm tree near the front door. I had decided to surprise him. It worked too well. He wasn't home. His place was tied down like a ship—windows boarded, garbage cans all gathered up inside the garage, even the mailbox pulled up and taken in.

I drove out across the new bridge to St. Pete Beach to find Junior. The bridge was still open, but I was the only one on it. At least Dottie's looked the same, except for a Coors Lite neon sign above the door. We never heard of Coors then, light or heavy. I saw several cars and trucks in the parking lot. Dottie's was not one of your sissy open-air bars; it was built of concrete block, sunk for some reason into the landfill, almost like a bomb shelter. It had only a few opaque blocks where its tiny windows might have been. Dottie's drinkers knew why they'd come, and it wasn't to get a suntan.

Regular drinkers are among the last people to permit a disruption of their schedule, even by acts of God. I'd seen the old pensioners live out what was left of their lives while I was first testing mine. They'd assemble promptly at ten P.M.—some of them still in military khaki, insignia removed but starched and creased—and fall out at two A.M., wrinkled and quietly shit-faced, when Dottie yelled "Last call for alcohol." Some of them started with beer and tomato juice. Some of them got a little wild now and then and ordered a glass of port to pour into their beer to make a Sneaky Pete. You couldn't get whiskey at Dottie's. Most of her patrons were happy with straight beer anyway. If you spaced it out and remembered to eat a ham sandwich now and then, it would get you through the day. There were bar snacks, there was sometimes TV, there was conversation. And sometimes there'd be a fight. Maybe it wasn't an exciting life, but you could count on it.

The three worn steps down into Dottie's often had the effect of launching the thirsty patron into the bar sooner than his dignity could withstand. After all these years, they got me again, and as I stumbled into the malty darkness, I heard Junior Huddle's voice, brassy and resonant with bitterness, before I could see him. "Bullshit," he was saying.

It echoed in the silence that followed my entrance. I couldn't see very well yet, but I knew all eyes were on me. "Congratulations, Mr. Huddle," I said in a game show host's voice. "You've just drunk your one millionth beer in this establishment. You win a liver transplant."

"Who the *fuck* are *you*?"

I followed Junior's voice down the bar to where he sat. My eyes were adjusting now.

"I'm Gat Sierra," I said, tired of acting nice. "I ran you right down the middle of that shuffleboard bowling machine one night when your mouth got away from you. We got a strike."

That bought me several seconds of silence and then Junior said: "Shit!" At least it was a change from Jesus. "Sonofabitch," Junior continued in that vein. "Last I heard you were killing gooks."

"It didn't work out very well. I was in the North Atlantic."

Junior had always been a small, spidery character, with long, thin arms and legs and almost no torso. He'd had a full head of black, wavy hair, slicked into a pompadour with Rose's Hair Oil. His hair was now a uniform battleship gray, but otherwise unchanged. It was the hair of a middle-aged male model, full and dignified; it was the hair of a banker; it didn't really belong on Junior. His face had the kind of tan that sick people get. His short waist had expanded outward to accentuate his spidery appearance. And maybe he had been spinning a web of a kind all these years, trying to keep Dottie's from changing, gathering victims for his poison, food for his ego, from the slower-moving barflies. "You here to drink?" he asked. He must have heard that I didn't.

"I don't drink anymore," I said, "but I want to buy everybody a refill." the old guys mumbled their appreciation while the pale, bald bartender hit his professional peak for the day. I put a ten on the bar.

"I'll buy my own," Junior said.

"I'm looking for Happy," I said. I figured it might go this way. Junior had always been bitter about anyone who left, or even changed. When I decided to go to college, he called me a fag, which was why I had bowled a strike with him all those years ago. I didn't actually get all of him in there, but his head and shoulders had tripped every pin.

"This ain't California," Junior said. "You may have noticed."

"I hoped you might have an address there. Did he write you?"

"Yeah. Maybe my secretary will be able to locate that correspondence. I'll just call her from my portable executive phone and have her look under Jesus freak. I think you're filed under private asshole."

"I'm beginning to feel like filing you again, Junior, right down in that strike zone."

"You wouldn't be gettin' no cherry," he said, flat, neutral, not caring either way.

"But I'll just run along," I said. The old guys mumbled their disappointment. "Jesus loves you, Junior."

"Oh shit," he said, real fear in his voice now. "Not you, too!"

Ten

I found Leila's in time to smell something good coming from the kitchen. She lived above a garage in an older section of downtown, northside St. Pete, about three blocks from the bay. She opened the door and smiled, and Junior Huddle's voice fell silent inside my head. "Will you eat meat?" she asked. "I got some steaks we could grill in case the power was out. I have a little fireplace."

"I'd probably eat a live armadillo tonight," I assured her.

"But the wind's so bad I'm afraid to open the flue, so I'll cook them inside. You want anything to drink?"

"I'd like to drag up my bags and take a shower."

"Drag away. I'll call you when it's ready."

We ate by the light of a real hurricane lamp, although we still had power. She told me the status of the storm hadn't changed. People were going crazy trying to figure out what it would do. She told me she was an Air Force brat, born at Hickham Field in Hawaii to an Anglo father and a Polynesian / Chinese / Portuguese mother and schooled mainly in Tampa, where he'd been transfered. I told her a little about myself. We sat in the dim light for a long time, talking and looking out at the storm. When the time came, it was as obvious and natural for us to make love as to sleep, which came much later.

Leila rewrote the book on the former, or changed what was too often a book to a kind of extended erotic dream. Every time I thought I'd found the end of her she showed me something new, a new urge, a new gratification, a new tenderness. She was a dream lover, a succubus, a love muscle. Coming off the peak of one of her surprises, I had a moment of unaccustomed stone-satisfied quiet in my mind and realized what old Mr. Rankaitis had been trying to tell me. I sat up. "Not St. Louis," I said, "*San Luis* Obispo. There's no way he could say Obispo. He probably thought it was the name of a state or something."

"You warned me you might act strange," Leila said, grinning. "Is this it?"

"Yes!" I said. "But trust me. It might make sense."

I looked up the area code for San Luis Obispo, a small city a little inland about halfway down California's coast. I rang information there and asked for Edward Allen Fox. Nothing. I cursed. Leila asked if she could help. "Do you have a good Atlas?" I asked.

She brought it back and I found two other San Luises in California—one, just a plain San Luis, near a reservoir of the same name in the northern San Joaquin Valley and the other a smaller place named San Luis Rey in the northern Sacramento Valley. The first one had no Foxes at all but the second had Edward Allen Fox.

I nodded at the operator. I grinned. I wrote it down. I explained to Leila what was happening.

"Is this how you solve cases?"

"Lots of times, yes. I could call the judge tomorrow. He'll probably have the address. I could get it other ways. But I think we have it now."

"We better check. It could be somebody else."

I thought about it. He wasn't running if he was in the book, but Sarah didn't want him to know about me or her until I could really check him out. We wanted to find out without giving ourselves away. "Are you ready for dramatics, subterfuge, spy stuff?" I asked Leila.

"Yeah," she said, smiling.

Leila played the secretary of one of our high school classmates who had become a banker and was now devoting his WATS line to locating all classmates for a possible reunion. That would allow her to ask anything within reason. And she did very well. It was earlier out west and Happy was still at work, but yes, his wife said, he had gone to that high school and would be interested in knowing what happened with the reunion. He would appreciate any mailing list that might result from this research. Yes, he had been out west in this location for several years now, running a garage and filling station. It was a family business. She was only home to start supper. He had two children, a boy and a girl. Actually, she was not the children's mother. Happy had remarried after the disappearance of his second wife. It was a great deal of information, more than we ever expected to get. Leila thanked the third Mrs. Fox, who asked God's blessing on her. She hung up the phone and filled me in.

"I don't know why I have to go out west," I said. "We can just ask them to make a family video for Sarah. Sounds good to me."

"You think Sarah would be satisfied?" Leila asked.

"I'll find out." I called Sarah and filled her in. She had just had an awful telephone row with Jennifer in Orlando, but she listened. "Do you want me to go out there?" I said.

"Yes," she said. "Unless you've changed your mind about spanking my daughter till her very expensive dental work rattles."

"No can do," I said. "But don't you think I've got

enough to satisfy us that he's O.K.?"

"From his third wife? The one who *didn't* disappear? Come on, Randy. Besides, I don't just want to be sure about him." Now, I thought, we will get to the real question, the only important investigation, and maybe a further small clue to the answers we hope *all* detective work will find for us. "I want to know what makes these bad things happen," Sarah said, "and how to make it stop."

"This is beginning to sound like a grail gig," I said. "I can't find the secret of life in a city directory."

"Do you mind going?"

I looked at Leila, beside me on the bed. "No, I guess not," I said. We said goodnight and I hung up. "I'm already packed," I said. "I've got a foam mattress and a sleeping bag, in case we can't find a decent motel."

"I've got a bag," she said. "I've also got a cooler and thermos, a camp stove, and some kits for cookin' and eatin'."

"Cookin' and eatin'," you say?

"That's right, dude," she teased, grinning up at me now from her pillow.

"So am I to understand that you're ready to motor west?"

"Motor," she said, giving it a new sound. "Take my way, it's the highway that's the best." Her grin was infectious.

We tried to sing it together, the Sammy Davis, Jr. version: "Get your kicks on Route 66."

"We *got* to go," she said. I was still laughing.

"Why's that?"

"Because the storm's bound to hit soon. Because I got two weeks off. Because you're finished here, except for me. And because we have a *lot* of *fun* together," she said.

Eleven

We were up early and there wasn't much to pack. I decided to go west with what I'd brought south—including a lot of gratuitous firepower—and buy the little extras I'd need. I planned to take I-75 north to Chattanooga, where we'd catch I-24 north for a while, then US 64 west to Memphis, where we'd join I-40. This was no time to travel the Gulf coast.

Leila brought a lot of tapes—good ones in the Best of category. Simon and Garfunkle; the Everly Brothers; Blood, Sweat and Tears; Fats Domino; The Band. We got off at Gainesville to visit a health food store she knew about and stock up on food she admitted was very pricey but which would save us from "crap on the road." I told her I didn't mind the occasional road crap—chicken-fried steak, iced tea already sweetened with refined sugar, country ham and eggs and grits and gravy, and truck-stop coffee—and she said the diet suited a man who carried no fewer than four loaded handguns. I told her that Jack Kerouac had recommended pie à la mode to me as the all-purpose On the Road meal, and she asked me how old he'd been when he died. The answer was forty-seven. I'd gone by to see him when I was at the junior college—just in time to watch him die.

We talked about Jack for a while. She knew who he was, but not that he'd died in St. Pete. Jack had been very much impressed by French bidets, and reflected that Americans—the earth's most frequent bathers and greatest consumers of deodorants—went around with what he called "dingleberries and dirty azzoles." She told me Americans had finally invented the portable bidet and showed me a cylinder of wet-wipes she'd brought along. Jack would have been pleased.

I remembered a line of his, burned into my memory by the fever of my adolescent hunger for the extraordinary. I recited it for her: ". . . the only people for me are the mad ones, the ones who are mad to live, mad to talk, mad to be saved, desirous of everything at the same time, the ones who never yawn or say a commonplace thing, but burn, burn, burn like fabulous yellow roman candles exploding like spiders across the stars and in the middle you see the blue centerlight pop and everybody goes 'Awww!'" Jack watched Neal Cassady, I told her, hoping to understand the madness, hoping to learn how to capture the flame and yet not be consumed by it.

"And you think maybe you'll learn it from Happy?" she asked.

I thought about it. "Maybe it is like that," I said.

We tried the airwaves. Some of the stations were doing what we'd already done—dump the Top 40 for oldies. But too often they tried to put even the oldies into a formula, a format, tried to chart the demographics, survey the market, capture their target audience. And the commercials were still done by guys with echoes in their heads. We listened to our tapes and sang along and caught "All Things Considered" and other NPR programs and those odd little stations beyond the reach of the Pop Machine. We tried to imagine that we weren't part of anybody's survey, that we belonged to no recognizable categories, that we were free.

We spent the first night in an unofficial camping spot I knew near a waterfall north of Atlanta, and the next in an Arkansas motel that offered "No Smoking" rooms with ashtrays and matches.

The rain had been almost constant since St. Pete. Still under David's influence, though he was reported to be petering out in the western Gulf. We made love in every state, sometimes in the car, sometimes in the open. It gave us something to look forward to, and thinking about it was more fun than radio or counting BMWs or even the old Burma-Shave signs. It called for ingenuity.

We played other games. We kept track of how often we sighted the same other travelers. I've often noticed the odd and distant sort of kinship that pilgrims on interstates develop with one another. It's not uncommon to see the same folks—the same family vacationers and loners and salesmen and long-haul truckers—all across the country; not uncommon to end up eating and sleeping in the same places and passing one another many times—often out of sheer boredom, everyone more or less in thrall to the 55 or 65 mph limit.

There was a family in a step van with open front doors. The van was all painted with California slogans and either a teenage boy or teenage girl was always hanging out of the passenger side as if about to deliver a milk order or hurl a newspaper. We kept worrying about the kids. We kept wondering how they kept up with us, since I had the radar detector and never drove under 70 and since they were lucky to have a top speed of 50. Maybe they got up earlier, or didn't stop as often or as early to fool around.

We lost them when we took I-35 north at Oklahoma City and picked up another westwarding group when we hit I-70 for Denver. We heard a show from a Tulsa station that made me nostalgic for Jim and Tammy Bakker. The broadcast was so slick that we didn't even know it was a religious station for a while. It's not so easy any-more to find the lonely, raving radio preacher with the breathy *ahhs* punctuating his phrases. These guys seemed as fully media slicked as Dan Rather. Money was in-volved. Somebody had a new theme park. Fun for all Christians.

I was fascinated. Leila hated it. "I got a theme park for those bozos," she said. "Raptureland, USA. We put 'em on one of those Morton-Theikol booster rockets and send 'em all to glory. James Watt can be the captain."

"I don't think they're all alike," I said. "Some of them are reacting to the same things we hate."

"Yeah, by censoring books, crippling the already fucked-over school systems, and voting for guys like Reagan and Watt, who think it's O.K. to turn the world over to corporate bandits because we're all going up to see Jesus soon anyhow."

"They're not all alike."

"I mean the fundamentalists."

"*They*'re not all alike. Some of them have been a civiliz-ing influence where no other good influence could reach. Like the South."

"Phoo," she said. "Where were those hairspray hypo-crites when we took sides over civil rights, the Vietnam War? Where are they on nukes, birth control, pollution, tobacco? Where are they in Central America? They've taken sides and they're the wrong sides. The good Chris-tians are giving sanctuary to refugees from the same 'freedom fighters' these blow-dry bigots want to support with our tax dollars. I say line 'em up and point the rocket at Uranus and blast 'em off to Rapture now before they do any more harm."

I let it go. I knew how she felt, but I also thought I understood how it must feel to be a guy with a family and some religious convictions surrounded by a world that looked more and more like Times Square. The rain had stopped, and Leila said she'd never seen so many stars. It was more open country and yet more of it was fenced, so we wouldn't be camping much until we got west of Denver.

The radio stations were doing something else that bothered us: trying to sell themselves to various workplaces, trying to get various parts of the labor force committed to listening to their station all day. They offered games and prizes, personal messages, a kind of flea market of the air. They seemed to see themselves as a morale booster, as the total morale picture for the poor bozos in the factories, warehouses, retail stores, even schools. What kind of work was being done by people who listened to the radio all day? Did this have anything to do with America's declining productivity, literacy, not to mention spirit? "That was Phil Collins for Mrs. Penny's Senior English Class at Wichita High, which is going to take a vocabulary test, right after this message from the Lineman Lounge." "And this one going out for all the gang at Missile Silo Three. Elton John and 'Rocket Man.'"

Leila and I goofed on the possibilities of a Radio Enslaved America. "Hey Fosdick, you wanta turn off that noisebox and check the console? Jesus Christ, look at them lights! Those are real missiles, people. They finally did it! We got incoming!"

"Stay tuned!" I yelled, in my best DJ echohead voice.

"Don't stay tuned," Leila yelled. "Everybody go outdoors and fuck!"

We played another game based on the premise that we had a radar device that would sterilize anyone we chose. We both realized that this game involved some dangerous assumptions, but we weren't serious.

"People with more than three visible, self-inflicted tattoos," I said.

"No argument there," Leila said. "People who have Bocephus bumper stickers on their trucks or cars or who have more than one Hank Williams, Jr., album."

"I like Hank. What about people who aren't actual cowboys but who wear cowboy hats."

"Wait a minute," Leila said. "Then we wouldn't have any more Willie Nelsons."

"Willie wears a bandanna. People who have a Phil Collins or Michael McDonald album."

"Hold on, Adolf. I've got a Michael McDonald."

"You didn't tell me that. I might have left you back in Florida."

"Lucky me. Here's one. How about people who have more than one handgun?"

We played another game. We'd noticed that the newer, cheap cars from abroad had ugly names like Hyundai and Yugo. The Japanese were offering computer-generated nonsense names like Camry. What's a camry? We Americans, afraid of falling behind in still another field, responded with names like Mercur. All of this sounded like graduation day at a Mongolian high school. Was it ugly they were after, or alien? We tried to help them out. "Kamikazi," I said.

"Balkar, from the planet Balpark," she said.

"Booger," I said.

"Smegma," she offered.

We continued in that vein for a while, driving through fields of sunflowers with their heads bent toward the sun like a poster in a mental health waiting room. "God, this is a great country," I said.

We caught a Sioux radio station, KILI, from "the Heartland of the Lakota Nation." We heard about community activities in the Wounded Knee School District and a picnic at Crazy Horse Park. "Be there or lose your hair," the announcer warned, and told us the rest of "what's happening on the res" before playing an Indian / country song called "I'm Gonna Live Without It, BIA," which must have had to do with the Bureau of Indian Affairs.

As we got closer to Denver we found KUBL, another

one of those little FM exotics near the far left of the dial. It played jazz, blues, and salsa. I taught Leila about scat, the station played Lambert, Hendricks, and Ross's "Everybody's Boppin'," and by the time we rolled into Denver late that night, we were trading eights on Dizzy Gillespie's "Night in Tunisia." Soobadabee zopzoboodee, soobadabee zopzabee, Soobadabee zopzoboodee, Zabeedabeedop doobee.

Twelve

We treated ourselves to a big hotel downtown—the Brown Palace, a room near the top. It was uncommonly clear and we thought we could see lights from the mountains above the glow of Denver. Leila hadn't really seen the Rockies yet, though we'd been climbing for many miles. Tomorrow she would. After a long shower, we made love on the carpet under the window. "You made me see stars," she said. I wished we could open a window and sleep above the smog, with the taste of approaching winter in the air. Windows don't open in modern hotels.

We walked around the next morning and found a cheap place for breakfast. We were standing on the street afterward, breathing smog and watching Denver traffic, when I saw the Kampground Killer drive by. He was on the other side of that one-way street, driving an older van—a small, tan one with screens over some of the windows and a pop-up top. He stopped at the light, in the far lane. It took me a few seconds to figure out where I'd seen him before.

When I did, I didn't yell. I just left Leila standing there and went for him, dodging traffic in the other lanes, which included a huge, white, Snap-on Tool truck. There was some brake noise and horn-blowing, which warned him that something was wrong. I had hoped to reach him without being spotted and open his door to grab the keys. I was coming from an angle behind and to the left of him, and he couldn't really see me until I rounded the rear of the Snap-on truck. But he twisted back to see what the noise was and saw me clear the truck and come for him. There was a split second in which I saw his confusion turn to recognition and during which I grabbed his door handle.

This guy kept his doors locked. Of course. And his window was up. He'd hit the accelerator without even checking the light or the road ahead, and he dragged me through a right turn—his luck was holding and I guess mine, too, because the light had changed and held traffic on that one-way street—before I gave up, dropped, and rolled almost under the wheels of a cab that had stopped for a more conventional fare.

I got up in time to read his Georgia tag before he reached the next corner, made a right against the light, and disappeared. I limped to the sidewalk, repeating the letters and numbers out loud. Several people came to stand around me. I opened the cabbie's jacket, took a ballpoint from his shirt pocket, and wrote the tag data on my left palm. I handed the pen back to him and said thanks. "This is police business," I told the crowd. "That man is a fugitive." It felt silly—like a street scene for a TV cop series—but everybody else seemed to like it.

Leila came running up—not a bit hysterical, considering—and began checking me for injuries. I was wearing some of Denver and it was wearing some of me. There was no chance of catching him now, so we went back to our room and chased the maids out. Then Leila gave me first aid from the kit we carried while I made some phone calls. The Denver police didn't seem to believe me. I gave them Romanello as a character reference and let them do what they would. I got a little more interest from the

Colorado Highway Patrol, who took the license data and description and asked me where I could be reached. I gave them Romanello's number and told them I'd drop by when I could. They were still trying to get a local address when I hung up.

I called Romanello and gave it to him quickly. I asked if he or the FBI could kick something loose before this guy stole another car and tag and was gone. He said he'd get right on it and to call him in a few hours. He gave me his home phone number in case he got a chance to go there. We said goodbye, both knowing how unlikely it was that anybody could react quickly enough—assuming this guy knew what he was doing. By the time the Denver police were on it, he'd be out of town; by the time the Highway Patrol decided he was hot, he could have stolen another vehicle and a different tag; by the time that vehicle was reported stolen or his old van was found, he'd be out of the state; and if I'd told the local cops where I was, I'd be eating Denver omelettes for a week before the smoke cleared. The guy could find another victim in that time. We packed, took the elevator down to the parking garage, drove around until we found I-25 north, and got out of town ourselves.

I hadn't planned to go north. I'd planned to stay on I-70 along the Colorado River for the scenery, then drive fast through Nevada on US 50. But north was the quickest way out of Colorado. Maybe he'd panicked, and if I'd seen him once, maybe I'd see him again. We seemed destined to cross paths. Fate is not logical. Certain people are brought together in defiance of any odds, as if they have some duty to perform for each other, owe each other some debt. This was beginning to sound like some New Age puffed brown rice, but I'd seen it too many times to argue with it. These days even physicists are getting downright mystical about probability, coincidence, things we used to measure with logic.

I had an officer in the Navy whom I swore I'd kill as soon as we were both discharged. Never mind why. I don't even remember. Why I thought I needed to wait I'll never know, because it's a lot easier to frag somebody on active duty—especially in special ops—than back in the world. We will never know how many unpopular salts now rest with Davy Jones, described to their survivors as "missing at sea" or "killed in the performance of his duty." Anyway, I thought I'd wait. Then one day I was walking along Times Square—where they say if you wait long enough you'll see everyone you ever knew—and saw him ahead. I could have killed him in the crowd and gone undetected. I was trained to do that. But he was talking to himself, and instead I walked behind him until I couldn't stand it any longer, forgave him—my charity undetected as he mumbled along with his ratty brief-case—and caught a cab.

But I wouldn't wait for this Kampground Krazy, this Ted Bundy striker with his all-American average, clean-cut, unmemorable appearance and his abbatoir of a psyche. If I saw him again, I planned to do more than sweep streets behind his vehicle. As I drove, I noticed the warning sign on my side mirror. I'd never thought much about it before. It read: THINGS ARE CLOSER THAN THEY SEEM.

Going north on I-25 we'd catch I-80 at Cheyenne and stay on it through Salt Lake City, across Nevada to Reno, where 50 met up with it, and all the way into Northern California. We were still south of Fort Collins when we began to hear sirens and at least a dozen state and county patrol cars passed us at very high speeds. I saw the last one take the turnoff at US 34 west and followed him the best I could without picking up a ticket until I saw an EMS vehicle pull off and followed him to where he was going for gas. It's times like these when I wish I'd bought the citizen's band and police scanner, the car phone, maybe even the TV. But it wasn't that hard to ask the EMS crew what it had heard to cause all the sirens. And the answer really didn't surprise me. "Somebody murdered three girls up in the Rocky Mountain National Park. Ranger just found 'em. Sounded real bad. Two other crews got the call and we heard some of the traffic. The FBI and the county ME are working on the scene. Nobody's bringing anything in. Not any time soon. Nobody's even got the parts sorted out yet."

I thanked them. We filled up, too, and I told Leila what they'd told me. "Should you go there?" she asked. I remembered warning her that this might take some bad turns, but it didn't make me feel much better.

"No. They already know what I know. They'll put it together with Romanello and the FBI. Every cop in the US wants that psycho. I'm hired to do something else."

The northern route turned out to be strangely relaxing; I was almost certain he hadn't run in this direction. When we crossed into Wyoming, Leila wondered, in light of how little of Wyoming we had to travel, if we'd make love in that state. I wondered silently, in light of the day's events, if we'd be in the mood. We wondered out loud about the strange, wooden barricades we saw at odd angles to the road. At a tiny gas station we asked the owner what they were. He was the first guy I'd seen who really looked like a cowboy. Lean, leathery, with those outdoor squint lines radiating from his eyes. There was an older man and a little tow-haired boy inside. The cowboy included them all in his answer:

"We tell some people they're bleachers for rodeos," he said. We nodded, waiting. "We tell other people they're tumbleweed collectors." We gave him some more time. "Or they might be fences for people who don't like to be fenced in."

It was my turn. "What do you tell people when you think they really deserve to know?"

"I tell 'em the truth," he said, pretending indignation.

"They're snow barriers. Government boys think they'll keep the snow from drifting onto the road."

"Do they?" Leila asked.

The cowboy grinned. "Right now they doin' just fine."

Everything was dry west of Denver. The radio told us how long it had been since it rained anywhere west of the Rockies. California's usual dry season was hotter and longer than usual, and there were fire warnings even along the Pacific Coast. Camping was now prohibited in many of the western states because of fire risk. We took it easy on ourselves and pulled off at Evanston, just before the Utah line, where we found a motel without a nightclub attached and where we could pay our erotic respects to Wyoming.

I'm sure we weren't the only folks who decided not to camp out for a while, although this guy, like Bundy, only chose women who were on their own. I'm also sure that women continued to camp alone or in groups all across the country, not so much because they didn't get the word as from the maddening blindness that makes horror pictures work—the assumption that it only happens to other people. We've all seen it: The lonely girl hears on the radio about the escaped Ginsu knife murderer, then walks outside in her negligee (aptly named) to investigate a noise. *Stay inside*, we're all thinking. He's *out* there.

I called Romanello at the department. "We passed it," I said.

"Maybe you should have stopped."

"You know how it gets. I couldn't have helped anybody."

"They want to talk with you," he said, sounding guilty.

"Oh, no," I said. "Don't tell me."

"I tried to tell the feds that you couldn't be involved, but one of those guys studied psychology. Said it was too coincidental, your being involved and near both scenes. He said maybe you're just making up this other guy and enjoying the show. They wanted your tag number and car description. I didn't have it. They'll get it through North Carolina."

"Christ."

"So you need to go in."

"But Leila saw him," I said, knowing already that it wouldn't help.

"She saw somebody," Romanello said tiredly. "You're the only one with a theory about who he is."

"Some thanks I get for being a good citizen. Thank you, Mr. Samaritan, now please bend over."

"I'll do what I can to get you out of there as fast as I can, but you'll have to talk with them. Where are you?"

"Fat chance. I'm getting a good night's sleep and then I'll go see the boys at Salt Lake City. Call Rueben Coffey, will you? Ask him to put in a few good words. Maybe Sheriff Hubbard?"

"You won't have any trouble," he said, in a voice that didn't believe him. "But it might take a while."

I said goodnight. Our room offered a hard-core movie option—last chance, pardner, before Utah—but we'd already heard too much about naked bodies that day, bodies somebody was still trying to sort out back there with floodlights and flashbulbs and plastic bags. Now somebody with a law or accounting degree and a lot of psychology courses thought I'd done that. I told Leila and we tried to laugh at the FBI. We didn't keep anybody awake with our hilarity. We'd only known each other about a week, and here was a fairly serious test.

She did fine. She really didn't seem to believe I was a killer, and I could almost accept the idea myself. We turned the AC thermostat way down, crawled under the covers, and made love like Mormons. Then we slept close, spooned together and holding each other to keep warm—as if winter were already upon us and a blizzard were piling up against the barriers, all along the Oregon Trail.

Thirteen

I didn't even get a chance to turn myself in. We were only a couple of miles into Utah when trooper pulled me over. He was polite; I'll give him that. He asked for all my paper and then asked me to get out of the car and cuffed me. He read me my rights. Leila got out and he read her hers, too.

"I k*now* my rights, Brigham," she said. "You just better make sure *you* don't forget 'em."

He called for a backup and spare driver, and they didn't take long. Not one of these guys was under 6'3"—two blonds and a brunet. Leila was just barely under control. She'd heard about the pigs from her Eckerd radical friends. Now here they were. I was glad they didn't decide to cuff her. To her they were Mormon versions of the SS; to me they were just the guys who were going to take me to where the real trouble was. They got a call back from the FBI and removed my cuffs. "Sorry," the trooper said.

I rode with one; Leila rode with another; the third drove my car. Mine didn't seem to want to talk, but I could see Leila jawing hers good in the unit ahead. He'd be getting an overview of the American system and potential threats to it. Then we'd get there and they'd search my baggage and find all my guns. I was glad the troopers hadn't searched me; of all the branches of law enforcement, they've probably suffered the most from the American tendency to drive around armed. And state troopers, by and large, are the last guys you want to try your badmouth on. I saw a little Washington state trooper go onto an Amtrak football train once and drag out an enormous drunken lawyer in a billy choke hold. The conductor, a local cop and a sheriff's deputy had been arguing with the guy for almost an hour. He'd threatened them with all the world's legal trouble. The trooper threw him head first against a stanchion in the train station to knock him out and asked if there was any more trouble.

"No," the conductor said.

"All aboard, then," the trooper said. "Which of you wants to book this clown?"

They took us to the Federal Building in Salt Lake City and to separate interrogations. I met agent Bell, a tired-looking, beefy, black man, and agent Linville, a little, red-haired guy with a rooster look about him. I hate little guys who are trying to be tough. You see a lot of that in DAs' offices. I'm all for tough prosecution, but not as theater or therapy for people trying to prove their manhood. Bell seemed disinterested, but Linville gave me his cold hand, then sat down, sneered, and said: "The only living witness. That's you."

"That's the title of a book about Ted Bundy," I said.

He let his eyes register sarcastic surprise. "You a student of Mr. Bundy?"

"Are you?" I asked.

"Yes. I'm a psychologist. I want to work in Behavioral Science—that's mass murderers—which brings us back to you."

I started to play the game with him, but stopped myself. "I don't want to get started wrong with you," I said. "I don't want to be a smart-ass. I'm not Jim Rockford and I don't have anything against law enforcement in general or the FBI in particular. I—"

"You're here to answer questions," he said.

"I'm not under arrest?"

"Not now. We just want to know about this series of coincidences."

"You cuffed me. You Mirandized me."

"The cuffs were a mistake," Bell said in a more friendly tone. "The Miranda was just in case. We're asking your cooperation as a witness." Good cop, bad cop.

"How about Leila?" I asked. "She's a writer and a friend of mine, along on another case. I know she's scared now and I want to reassure her."

"What's she got to be scared of?" Linville said.

I put the question to Bell: "Let's do this right. Bring her in here and tell her exactly what the deal is. Make it clear that she doesn't have to talk to you. Ask her to be a friendly witness. Let me reassure her. We don't have anything to hide."

Linville snorted and looked away. Bell caught his eye and then left the room for a while. It was a government all-purpose meeting room, with a steel table, minimally padded chairs and walls painted with a greenish-white paint the government must have bought a lot of at one time. I've seen it a lot. And smelled it. It smelled like something developed to tame Vietnamese jungles. After you'd been around it for a while you realized that you'd developed a habit of holding your breath and breathing only when you had to.

Linville stared at me for a while. I stared back. He looked upward and to the right at the greenish white, malodorous wall, as if asking it to witness my folly. "Are you going to talk to me?" he asked finally.

I still thought I could keep it from getting personal. He was lame. He probably hadn't been in the field very long and thought this was the way to do it. Or maybe he'd been in the field too long and was burning out. He wanted to work at Quantico, in Behavioral Science, and if they wouldn't let him hunt mass murderers, maybe he'd find me on his own, as an ordinary field agent. Maybe if I just gave him a little more reason to feel secure.

"Yes, I am," I said. "I want to reassure the girl. And I want to ask my client's permission to talk about why I'm out here."

Bell brought Leila in, interrupting one of Linville's best sneers. "I'm not talking to these three-piece assholes," she said. Bell tried to hide a smile. Linville began working on a sneer for her.

I stood and took her hand. Bell put a chair under her and she looked at him suspiciously before she sat in it. "Let's not do it that way," I said. "These are FBI agents and we have nothing to hide." Another agent leaned in and Linville went to the door to confer with him in a whisper. The whispering distracted Leila, who was more frightened under her bluster than I realized. She looked over her shoulder at them and I held my explanation until I could get her attention.

Linville turned to me. "Permission to search your vehicle and baggage?" he said to me.

Leila looked back at me. She was really scared now. "Granted," I said. "There are four handguns in all. All registered."

Linville raised his eyebrows, then turned and nodded to the other agent and returned to his seat across the table from me, rubbing his hands. "Go on with what you were saying about not having anything to hide," he said.

"I was taking those pistols to a gunsmith in Florida for modifications and sighting. The hurricane prevented my doing that."

Leila had dropped her head and was staring at her lap. I reached out and raised her head gently. "It's all right," I said.

"You mess up any of my stuff, you'll pay for it," she told Linville. She was hanging between bluster and despair, and I figured it was safer to keep her on the bluster side. She could fight with Linville. It would keep her courage up.

"Let's do the questioning here," I said to Bell. "I've leveled with you, agreed to talk, let you search our stuff. There's no reason to question us separately."

Linville wanted to play with that, but Bell was tired and said: "Let's talk with them here." He looked at Linville as if to say let's cut the shit and Linville adapted to it without showing too much chagrin. They brought me a phone and I dialed Sarah.

I didn't want to scare her, so I did a little small talk, asking her about the hurricane, which had finally wound down and come ashore in Texas without doing too much damage, and telling about our trip. My trip. This didn't seem like a good time to mention Leila. Jennifer was back from Orlando and seemed uncommonly happy and busy with something she hadn't had time to explain. Jean-Pierre sent his best. I could hear Linville chewing up the minimal padding on the steel chair with his butt cheeks. Then I heard him snort, and then he farted. It was a loud one, a ripper. Hearing this last I asked Sarah to wait and turned to him as if to say Please, I'm on the phone. His already beety complexion deepened. I looked at Bell in a silent appeal for him to control his partner and Bell fought to control himself. Leila didn't try. She giggled.

Farting is universal. It comes to meek and mighty alike, the great windy leveler. Coming at the right time, in the right pompous circumstances, it's the one thing we all think is funny. Except the flatulent. Or is it the flatulant? Anyway, if you're trying to be a hard-ass, you've got to watch your diet. And this one had an odor to it. Worse than the paint. I looked over at the wall as if wishing it had a window. Bell got up and opened the door to our interrogation room. A loyal partner might not have done that. Linville would either be a lot easier to deal with now or a lot nastier. I heard Sarah's anxious voice from the phone. "What's going on?" she asked.

"Something came up," I said, and Leila giggled again. "Look, the FBI wants to question me about that creep I saw on the road in Florida. I saw him again out here. To answer them I need your permission to talk about this case."

She was silent for a few beats. "Sure, I guess," she said. "Is this kind of thing usual?"

"Very usual, very ordinary," I said. "Nothing to worry about."

"Go ahead then, and good luck," she said. "Where are you?"

"Salt Lake City."

"Geez, I've never been there. Is it pretty?"

"I hear it's beautiful, but so far I haven't seen much beyond these government-issue walls; green, malodorous." I named the punctuation marks, emphasized the malodorous.

"Well, at least see the Tabernacle and the lake," she said. "And call me after you see Happy."

I promised I would. Bell got up to close the door and we had our interrogation. Linville had modified his sneer somewhat and when Bell was called out continued questioning Leila and me with a kind of detached resignation. He didn't even seem too surprised or disappointed when Bell came in and told us that the van I'd described had been found parked on a residential street in Evergreen. Initial reports suggested that it had been well scrubbed, but the forensics boys from Washington were finished at the campground and were being taken over to examine the van. Maybe they'd find a partial print, a microscopic spot of blood or skin or hair, a strand of fiber.

A Bronco had been stolen in Evergreen. By now it had a new tag, the first of several if our man was as smart as he seemed. And he wouldn't keep the Bronco long. Maybe he'd steal a cooler vehicle and cover his tracks before he had to kill again. He probably wouldn't go west, considering the fire hazard, or north, with winter coming. Or maybe that's exactly what he'd do. Bell shared all of this with us in a way which suggested we were no longer under suspicion. Linville stared at the wall in a way which suggested he was no longer interested—in the case, in us, in life. Bell thanked us and Linville just sat there while we left.

Bell led us down to the parking garage carrying a cardboard box containing my various documents, keys, and firearms. He thanked us and headed for the elevator. Leila didn't like the way the feds had handled our suitcases, so we spent some time repacking everything. We'd gotten in and started the engine when Linville appeared before us, glaring over the hood. He walked around to my side and I rolled down the window.

He'd restored himself somehow and was nastier than ever. He just stood there for a while, scowling like a gargoyle. "It could still be you," he said finally. "There are two of you. You could have done it, using both cars."

"It doesn't make sense," I said, still hoping for peace. "No two psychos could work together to commit crimes like these."

"What about the Hillside Strangler? Two guys. Or maybe she's lying to protect you."

"Why would I do murders and then call attention to myself by reporting somebody I think was the murderer?"

"For excitement. To make the police look stupid. Like Bundy."

"I get enough excitement. I do this for a living."

"I'm running a background check on you," he said.

"Does Bell know about that?"

"I don't need his permission. I'm still on your case. I want you to check in every week."

"I won't do that," I said.

He paused. I know he wanted his next line to be right. The pause got the better of him and he rushed it. "Keep you nose clean," he said.

"And you better check your shorts," Leila said.

Fourteen

"Thank you very much," I said to Leila. We were downtown, trying to find the Tabernacle. "I get lazy and don't really enjoy every moment to the fullest unless I've got the FBI hunting me for mass murder."

"I'm sorry. I was scared. Sometimes when I'm scared I get belligerent. And with a nasty mouth. It surprised me, too."

"A regular Bonnie Parker."

She giggled. "Why is this an FBI case?" she asked.

"At first it was only because it was assumed that whoever killed the girls in Florida had left the state. The FBI gets involved in interstate flight to avoid prosecution. That was a state park, you see, and if they'd caught a suspect, it would all be a county and state show. Murder itself is not a federal crime. But the FBI does tend to get involved in really serious crimes if it seems the investigation might lead beyond the bounds of the original jurisdiction. And they help local cops sometimes if they're asked. But this last one was a national park, so it's in their primary jurisdiction, although they'd have to arrest him for interstate flight or violation of civil rights or something, and let the states prosecute him for murder. It's also clear by now that we have the same MO in all three cases."

"Then they oughta catch him soon, with all their computers and stuff."

"Not necessarily. They can chase him from state to state, true, and they have access to the big picture. But they have a reputation with a lot of local and state cops for being pretty nine-to-five, much better at catching bank embezzlers through audit than with hot pursuit. The agency recruits lawyers and accountants. They get a white-collar kind of agent."

"So maybe Linville is so lame he won't even bother you any more."

"A lame with a badge can be a lot of trouble. Let's just hope he was having a bad day. Maybe he'll get a decent meal and find somebody to haul his ashes and forget all about me. Probably somebody in Reno would give odds on that, but I think I already know how slim they are. Our best hope is that they catch that hacker."

I found the Tabernacle and a short-term parking space not too far away. We got out to play tourist, holding hands and gazing up at the magnificent product of Joseph Smith's strange dream of the prophet Mormon. If I'm not mistaken, there was an angel named Moroni involved somewhere along the way, too. I've thought from the first time I heard of them that Smith could have used some help naming the characters in his drama—including himself. Any good political image-maker could tell you that nobody's going to suffer ridicule, persecution, and murder—from Palmyra, New York, through the long, cruel exodus west to this magnificent high desert—for a guy named Smith and a prophet named Mormon.

We drove along Salt Lake. It was clear and we could see the Rockies rising behind the city. It was a lovely day and it was good to be out of that poisonous government room with a pretty girl and a full tank and a radar detector and a whole, flat state ahead patrolled by troopers who thought 55 mph was as silly as I did. I didn't drive as fast on I-80 as I could have on old US 50, but we did some motoring.

Then I saw a chance to avoid the unnecessary northward loop the interstate made and took state road 278 at Carlin down to 50 where it crossed at Eureka. We really made some time through the desert. There was almost no FM reception out there, and the AM stations were either of the country or the more hysterical, hydrophobic religious sort. It was dark long before we got to Reno. We should have left the radio off. A local station was playing the Doors' oldie, "Riders on the Storm." Just right for a season of highways and storms and cold murder. A golden oldie, still fresh, always appropriate in our road-hungry and deadly republic.

"Where will we stay tonight?" Leila asked. We were back on I-80 and we'd passed one Reno exit already. I wanted to push on toward the Donner Pass and sleep under the stars in some unofficial camp spot, but it seemed plain that Leila wanted to stop here. "I've heard one good thing about casino hotels," I said. "That they build them for quiet because people keep weird hours and want to be sure they've got a quiet place to sleep."

"I've never been in a casino," she said.

"Then we'll stop and take a look. It's almost our bedtime, but things are just starting to cook there."

"On the other hand, this might be our last chance to camp someplace nice. Aren't the Sierras just a little farther?"

"Sure are." I missed the next exit. "There's a place I found years ago on the Truckee between here and Lake Tahoe. It might be condos now, but then again maybe it's still there. If it isn't, something else will be. We'll stay away from official campgrounds. It's better that way anyhow. We can sleep under the stars."

"And can we wash in the river tomorrow morning?

Use our camp stove? We haven't done that yet."

"Sure."

"Pull off here."

I thought she'd changed her mind and just barely caught the last Reno exit, a little disappointed. But she wanted an all-night market, and a coffee pot and real coffee, and bacon and eggs, corned beef hash, catsup, and a loaf of Roman Meal bread, and even a small stick of real butter and some ice to keep it cool.

"This is quite a departure for us," I said. "We've been living pretty close to the natch here, and frankly I'm surprised."

"School's out," she said. "I got a taste for grease. If the pioneers could get by without granola, so can we."

We found the place I remembered from years ago. I don't know how it dodged the developers. I don't really know how I remembered or found it again; I'd been eating mushrooms on that last trip, with an actress from L.A. Maybe there was some magic in the place. We were able to drive the car right down to the river. A cooking fire didn't seem a big risk so close to the water, and I'd bank it with gravel and stones from the river and drown it before bedtime. We had hash and eggs for supper, with bread and butter and coffee. We even had some cheese-cake which Leila had bought secretly when she went back for a paper. I glanced through the paper by flash-light as we sipped coffee. KAMPGROUND KILLER STRIKES IN COLORADO. The New York *Post* would probably spell Colorado with a K. I offered the paper to Leila and she shook her head. "It was just an excuse for the cheese-cake," she said. "I didn't come out here to read bad news." I crumpled it up for morning kindling.

We washed the dishes by flashlight and moonlight, with Truckee sand and a biodegradable soap Leila had bought in Gainesville. Coyotes called from across the river. We decided against sleeping on the ground because of snakes, but I reversed our bedding in the back of the Eagle so that we'd be able to look up from where we slept and see the stars. It had been so hot for so long crossing the desert that it took us some time to realize how cool it was here. I took some towels down to the beach and we waded in by moonlight and washed each other with that same soap. Then we made love on the bank—like Indians, we hoped—washed off again in the cold river, toweled each other, climbed in back, brushed the sand from our feet, and huddled shivering together in the bag—flashlight and .45 handy, beneath the western sky.

Fifteen

The sound of the river was so peaceful that we slept through several hours of daylight before starting a leisurely morning routine. We used the camp stove for coffee, bacon and eggs. It was hard to believe this place had been left alone. It hadn't. As we reached the hard road I saw the sign we'd missed in the dark. A SOLD banner had been slapped over a FOR SALE sign. There was a Plymouth Voyager van parked near it, and a woman in a quilted jacket and two men in windbreakers gazed at us in puzzlement as we passed. By tonight there would be two treated four-bys sunk and a chain stretched across the road. By next week the access road would be cleared and graded and they'd be marking streets and septic tanks and getting some juice wired in for lights and saws. There'd be a cute sign with a Logo: Tahoe Run, Truckee Bank, Donner Pasa. Leila suggested Two Indians Fucking. Or maybe White People Eating One Another. I knew I didn't want to go back and find out.

I have a strange instinct for finding good places. Lately I seem to find them just ahead of the boosters and boomers and progress brokers. I keep moving to these lovely, quiet spots and finding myself overrun within a year by gravel trucks and construction pickups. Maybe I bring them somehow. Maybe they've got me wired and I don't know it. I've learned to see it coming and keep moving. I know the signs better. I'm like the canary in the mineshaft; when I can't breathe, the rest of you better look out. Or maybe it's just happening everywhere now, during the old Boomer Regime's Last Roundup and Big Bidness Barbeque. The business of Business is busyness. Maybe when this generation of boomers has spent itself—how will they jump from windows in these modern buildings?—some of us will come back to reclaim this land and maybe even modify these buildings and live in some spooky parody of the '80s.

We came down from the Pass into a northern valley dry and ominous as a rattlesnake. The Reno DJ had not been an isolated case; everybody was playing "Riders on the Storm," which seemed a weird and typically American tribute to the Kampground Killer, who had butchered and raped another girl in the Natchez Trace State Park in western Tennessee. The Doors oldie was in the Top Twenty and climbing.

While people west of the Rockies sensibly feared fire and many jurisdictions had banned camping and hunting until the rains came, easterners who had survived several hurricanes now shivered in delicious horror at news of the Kampground Killer. But the song was on all the stations out here, too. School had started weeks ago, but it still felt like summer, as if autumn and winter and our saner business were being held back by these natural and unnatural summer dangers. We took 20 through Grass Valley and over to I-5, then north for a while and west on another state road. By early afternoon we were in San Luis Rey.

It was a nice enough little town. Most of its business seemed related to farming, trucking, lumber from the mountains to the west. We drove along an industrial strip for a while, admiring the farm equipment and truck washes. Then there was a little old-fashioned commercial strip with Dairy Queens, donut shops, an older diner built like a house trailer. Maybe they'd put all their newer franchise fast-food places on the other side of town. We turned where a sign pointed to downtown, still buzzing from the road, grateful for the Eagle's air conditioning, a little slow witted.

I pulled in to a gas station to fill up and get my bearings. Leila hadn't asked his wife where Happy worked and I'd have to call and get it from her now. A wiry man in a Texaco shirt smiled into my window and said, "Fill her up, sir?" I grumbled that I'd apparently come to the wrong set of pumps and that I'd back up and find the self-serve island. "This is it, sir," he said. "Let me do it for you. I've got some spare time. No charge." I was surprised to encounter such uncommon courtesy, surprised also to see the lovely girl take over the gas hose while the man went around to poke under my hood for the latch they can never find. I made sure the cable was pulled, then got out, walked around to help him find the latch, read Ed on his striped shirt, and realized who he was. He didn't know me; but then he wasn't looking for me.

Leila had recognized him before I did, though I don't know how. She was pointing at him from behind the windshield. I nodded that I understood and she beamed. It was a luxury, those few seconds. The unknown visitor, the friendly ghost. The girl at the gas pump looked like an angel in a Texaco shirt. The station was spotless, like something from 1955 or the set of a Spielberg movie. These people didn't care that the American people had been trained to pay more for pumping their own gas and holding their bladders and driving away with the reek of gas on their dirty hands. They gave you clean restrooms and soap and towels and smiles because they thought that was the way it should be and they wanted to do it.

Another car pulled up and the girl went to tend it,

setting the handle to slow-fill on mine. I watched Happy's face as he checked my oil, brake fluid, water, then called out to Leila to start it so he could check the transmission fluid. It wasn't necessary, but it gave me time to watch him. His face was fuller but he was still lean. He brought a kind of concentration to his various tasks that was attractive and soothing to watch. I could probably call Sarah right now and report that Happy Fox was doing fine. But she wanted more and so did I. "Looks good," he said, closing the hood carefully with a red garage rag to avoid smudges. He looked up and something passed over his face. He shrugged it off and started back to finish the pumping. "You're a long way from Dottie's, aren't you, pilgrim?" I said to his back. He turned slowly and his mouth opened. His eyes darted up and down me. He closed his eyes and lowered his head and nodded it. Then he came toward me and I held out my arms. It didn't seem awkward as it had with Petey. But there was one more surprise: Leila had watched me being questioned as a suspected mass murderer; now she'd have to see me wet eyed and red faced for a while. And Happy, whose face she'd last seen in a mug shot.

We recovered, tough guys that we were. The angelic blonde was confused. Leila got out and introduced herself to the girl. It didn't clear anything up, but it was a friendly gesture. "I'm Rebecca," the girl said.

Happy and I were having trouble figuring out what to say, or maybe we were just buying time so that we'd be able to say whatever it was without another scene. Leila was carried away by the whole thing. She hugged me and then hugged Happy, which made the cover story I'd decided on sound hollow. I wish Leila and I had thought to work it out in advance. Now she seemed to know who everybody was. Maybe Happy wouldn't think critically about it. Sarah wanted me to have an honest look, and it wouldn't work if I told him why we were here.

"I can't believe it's you," he said. His voice had the same raspy quality. It still sounded more like the voice of a nose-puncher than a preacher. "What brings you here?"

I warned Leila off with my eyes and I don't think Happy noticed it. Most of us would hardly expect somebody to drive across a continent to see how we're doing. "Unbelievable coincidence," I said, which was not exactly a lie. It was unbelievable, though I hoped he would believe it.

"I've thought of you so often," he said. "Somebody called a while ago about a reunion. Imagine us having it here." He turned to the girl. "Honey, please go call Martha. Ask her if Chris is home and can come to help out. It's time for his shift anyway. If he isn't, ask her to come. That way we can talk." He turned back to me and the girl ran into the station. "Can you stay a while? Can you come have supper tonight?"

"Sure," I said. "We were heading for the coast in a general way. Maybe drive up through the redwoods into Oregon. No special plans. We can check into a motel and spend some time here."

"Chris isn't home," the girl called from the office. "Do you want Martha to come?"

"No," Happy said. "Ask her to stay on and I'll come talk to her. This is great," he said to me. "I'll close here early, at five. Business is slow anyway." He wrote a number on a blank credit card slip. "Call us here about five-thirty and come over at six. Wait a minute. Don't get a motel. You can stay with us."

"Thanks," I said, "but this also happens to be a business trip. We're on expenses and I've got to make some phone calls. It would be easier on everybody if we just found a room."

"The Mission Adobe is nice," he said. "Good, Christian couple owns it. Sure you won't stay with us?"

"No, but we can stay in town a while. Thanks anyway."

"Martha can start cooking something special," he said. Two more cars pulled in at the same time. He hung the hose back onto my pump and I reached for my wallet. "On the house," he said. He went for one car and Rebecca took the other. He still moved well. I tried to imagine him reaching in to hit, jamming the driver with the door as he tried to get out. I couldn't. He got the pump going and ran past us for the office. He stopped at the door, turned, shook his head, and smiled. "This is no accident," he said. "This is Providence."

Sixteen

We took a look at the Mission Adobe and decided to try it. The managers were a Chinese couple, neither of whom seemed to speak much English but who communicated somehow, mainly through smiling and saying "yes" or "no" to our questions. We assumed this was the Christian couple Happy mentioned. Maybe they all belonged to the same church, or Happy's church brought them here from Vietnam or Mainland China. We got the room all the way back on the top, with a plant nursery behind. We registered as Mr. and Mrs. Joseph Smith and Leila thought that was funny as hell. I decided not to call Sarah until we knew more, so we showered the dried salt from our bodies, made love and took a nap, the air conditioner making a friendly hum.

I called Happy around five-thirty and got directions. He lived at the end of a cul-de-sac beyond which we could see dry, brown hills, rocks, and a few bushes that already looked burned. Here and there we saw a crow perched on one of those seared bushes, his prehistoric-looking beak opened, as if panting. I remembered my friend, Andy, who had evacuated his little cabin in Simi Valley for three years running only to have the fire pass him by. Then, when the call came the fourth year, Andy thanked the warden and told his wife, "You can leave if you want, I'm not going to waste another Sunday," and stayed to drink Scotch and watch football until the firestorm took him. The land beyond Happy's looked like that. There were probably Indian markings on the rocks. It was hard to believe it ever showed a spot of green. It was Biblical looking and I imagined Happy liked that. Living in a three-bedroom ranchette next to land like that the Israelites had wandered was having cake and eating it too.

But something was wrong at Happy's house. Everybody made us welcome, but there was an undercurrent of alarm which I figured had something to do with the absence of the son, Christian. Happy's newest wife, Martha, was dark haired, petite, and pretty in a sharp-featured way. She had the kind of face that was almost too perfect. There was nothing in it to suggest relaxation or spontaneity; my guess was that she always looked a little worried, although she seemed to have some reason now. Her voice was surprisingly vibrant and her speech was perfectly articulated. She sounded like a lady preacher, which no doubt she was. Like her face, the voice rarely relaxed, and so conveyed a feeling of tension.

The house was modestly furnished and immaculate. It felt comfortable, like the home of a real family, even if it was a troubled one. Happy walked us through it the way hosts always seem to do. Like most hosts, he skipped his own bedroom. We saw Christian's room, which seemed a little too neat for a teenager, even a Christian one. Rebecca's had flowered wallpaper, a dresser and mirror but no makeup, a map of the Holy Land, and a bookcase filled with books and with a small aquarium on top. There were guppies in it, the males displaying bright tails in their constant pursuit of the perpetually pregnant females. I wondered if goldfish might be more appropriate. On a night table next to her bed was an ancient portable record player with a speaker in the cover. Most kids wouldn't be caught dead with such low-tech gear, but Rebecca wasn't most kids. Under the table were some albums, the first by Amy Grant, the second by Paul Simon. I picked a book from the case. It was a biography of St. Theresa of Avila, published by a Catholic press. She also had the classic eleventh edition of *Britannica*. A kid could learn what he or she needed in a home like this.

But it wouldn't be easy. All through the living room were pictures of the family. There was only one of the children's mother, a smiling, big-boned blonde who wore in this photo a karategi. "We're a karate family," Happy said proudly. "We belong to a Christian dojo. Everybody's a black belt except Martha, and she's testing for green belt next week." Martha tried to look enthusiastic about it, but it was clear she was a reluctant convert to the martial arts spiritual path. I had the feeling she might rather have been tortured in a more Biblical way.

Chris was a good-looking blond boy, maybe a year older than Rebecca. He was pictured in Little League, school photos, in karategi in a fighting stance, and passing out pamphlets at a Motley Crue concert. Not an easy mix for a teenage kid with the surfer good looks that would get him any of California adolescence's easier prizes. There were several photos of him and Rebecca at various ages and one of him and Happy sparring in a stagey kind of way for the camera. "We're expecting Chris for supper," Happy said. "Now let's sit down and catch up on things."

Martha excused herself and went to the kitchen to continue cooking. She didn't move her body when she walked; her legs switched back and forth precisely, like scissors. Rebecca and Leila went out and offered to help her—Leila bowing on this occasion to traditional sex roles—but she sent them back in to join us. She came to sit with us between tasks. She didn't seem entirely comfortable there but didn't want to miss it, either.

"Did you ever get involved in this?" Happy asked, pointing to the karate pictures.

"I did a lot of it in the seventies," I said. "I was moving around and so I trained in different styles. I did a lot of tournament fighting. Got one of those Lenox-Hill braces for my knee."

"How far did you go?" Rebecca asked.

"I earned dan rank in two different styles."

"Don sounds Spanish," Leila said.

"Dan is black belt," Happy explained. "It's usually pronounced like 'don' but spelled like 'dan.'" He turned to me. "Good for you," he said. "You always had talent."

I smiled. "I just didn't have the killer instinct."

"Some of us thought we had it and didn't," he said.

"I'd like to know more about all of that," I said, but maybe it wasn't the right time. We did some catching up about parents and old friends. His and my parents were gone. I told him about visiting Petey, Aldo, and Junior. He shook his head sadly. I described the old neighborhood and my talk with Mr. Rankaitis. He listened like a man hearing a tale of what he did during a blackout. I told him a little about Sarah. He seemed quite charmed by that until Martha scissored into the room and took her chair next to him. Because he asked, I told him a little about my life.

"Someone wrote me that you were a Navy SEAL," he said, "and then that you were working for the Hillsborough sheriff. I heard some other things later." He let that go because there were ladies in the room. "I was thinking about going to the reunion," he continued. I couldn't figure a way to tell him that there wasn't going to be a reunion—that this was it. "I think it would be a real challenge seeing all those people if you had learned to live an . . . unconventional life. I mean I wouldn't go there and preach to them, but I don't think I could hide it, either."

"It would show in your face, Daddy," Rebecca said. "In the way you talked and walked. You'd be witnessing."

Martha nodded. "I told them you might come," she said. "It would be a shame to miss a chance to testify like that. You've got a light now that shouldn't be hidden."

I was afraid it would go on and get embarrassing. I was worried that they'd start trading Bible verses and I'd have to sweat and fidget like Huck Finn praying in the closet with Miss Watson. The worst part was it was all based on a lie I told them. But they simmered down. They'd probably talked it over and decided not to put too much religion onto outsiders at first. I wondered why it hadn't kept them from passing out those pamphlets at rock concerts. The sheer humiliation of it would have overwhelmed most of the baddest guys I've known.

Why is religion such an awkward thing for so many of us? Why should it make me sweat bullets to have someone quote the Bible or pray? Maybe it's because most of us have been trapped by those sad neighborhood canvassers or airport pamphleteers, wrapped in a web of desperate, sweaty, hot-breathed evangelism, paralyzed like a spider's victim, reluctant to exert that last burst of free will and say, like Coleridge's Wedding Guest, "Unhand me, greybeard loon!" And because most of us feel sorry for anyone fallen to such public degradation. And because most of us deep down consider ourselves the blackest sinners and may be right.

Supper was ready. We all carried something from the kitchen through the swinging door around the corner to the dining room table. Martha told us where to put it and where to sit. Chris's empty chair reminded us that something was wrong. Happy led us in a brief and pleasant prayer of thanks which ignored his absence, and we ate. Martha had learned to talk *and* cook in the South, and she had this wonderful harvest array of Big Valley California vegetables from which to choose. There was a ham, sure, but the veggies stole the show: salad greens, little red potatoes, green beans, candied yams, two kinds of squash, and even okra with tomatoes. And corn bread. Huck would have approved.

After dinner, we took our plates to the kitchen and found our living room chairs again. Rebecca tackled the dishes. They apparently didn't believe in coffee, but the house was air conditioned, so we were comfortable if a little groggy.

Strangely, it was Martha who undertook the narrative of Happy's life, like the tribal rememberer, the Gaelic *seanachaidh*, the Gospel according to Martha: "Happy was touched by God during the first year after his release from jail in Florida. He was walking on Redondo Beach, high on drugs and confused, not wanting to go back to the apartment where all his bad friends were. A man approached him to try to tell him about Jesus Christ." Martha made the words sound so rich and glorious I think they might have made Jesus himself blush. Happy was gazing into space, like a man listening to an inspirational tape. "He rejected the man, but something stayed with him. He often drove the streets or walked the beaches, hoping for an answer to his confusion and rage. One night he met Diane. His first wife had divorced him while he was in jail. Diane was hitchhiking and he picked her up. He asked her if she believed in Jesus Christ. She said she wanted to. She'd been a Christian but had lapsed and wanted to find God again. A week later they were married."

We sat and listened like one of those early congregations. Instead of the catacombs, we huddled in a California ranchette. "But they couldn't seem to get free of drugs," Martha continued. "One night Happy was lying in bed, miserable with guilt, when God spoke to him." Martha stopped and smiled at Happy. Apparently this was his part in the narrative.

"I read some of that in the paper," I said, not sure why I was interrupting, "but I'd like to hear you tell it now. It was after you'd left Florida that somebody showed it to me. I wanted to ask you about it, but nobody knew where you were."

"I was writing to most of them," Happy said. "I sent literature." We understood each other and let it go.

"It was the most wonderful thing," he continued. "I've often thought I'd like you to know about it, Gat, because of something I'll tell you later. It wasn't exactly a voice, an audible voice like mine or yours. But it was so *strong*, so definite and unmistakable. There was a presence in the room, and then that presence showed me that it was part of everything, that everything partook of it. All fear dropped away. It was the word you always yearned to hear but never thought you would. Not a measly, little, literal human word but the message, the secret, the *sense* and joy and glory of God. I knew I'd been touched by the only force that mattered, singled out for something special after all my sins. Maybe be*cause* of my sins. I knew that our ego-driven personality is as weak and ridiculous without God as a hand puppet without a hand. It was such an unexpected gift, a great privilege. I had a meaning in my life."

"Did it last?" I asked him. I'd had something like that during the worst of my drug withdrawal, but it had dimmed like a dream, and although it was overwhelmingly convincing at the time, I never thought of going out to preach.

He seemed to understand my question. "Not in that overpowering way," he said sadly. "Nobody could stand that much ecstasy. They'd have to lock me up for sure. It let me go so that I could live again in the real world and carry its message."

"What happened to Diane?" Leila asked.

This was Martha's subject again. "She disappeared

one day over five years ago and never came back. We never heard a word from her. After two years, Happy got a divorce on grounds of desertion." Martha said the word with a certain moral smugness, then went a little beyond. "She began to talk about white witchcraft, about living like the tribal hunter-gatherers, strange stuff. Maybe she's found happiness living with some tribe of bug-eaters in New Guinea. I'm sorry. That was unkind."

Right, Martha. A storm passed quickly across Rebecca's face.

"Chris had a hard time adjusting to it," Happy said. "Her absence. He kept thinking he could find her, bring her back to the fold. He doesn't realize how big the world is, how easy it is to become lost.

"Kids don't necessarily get divorced when parents do," I found myself saying, not knowing where I'd gathered that wisdom.

Happy let that sink in for a moment, then nodded. Rebecca let out her breath.

"I'd met Martha at a revival," Happy said, smiling again. "And in a way, you and your mother were responsible for this whole thing happening as it did."

That really surprised me. I couldn't imagine what my sweet and stubborn old mom could have had to do with this nest of piety, although no doubt she would have approved of it. He seemed to hesitate. Finally he said: "You remember that little Baptist church you went to?"

I nodded. My Kentucky mother had been adamant about saving my sister and me from the wiles of my dad's lapsed Catholicism. Dad never went to church and didn't mind at all what we did in a religious way, but Mother knew the Catholics were subtle and felt that we'd need a strong Protestant training to resist popery—even such indifferent popery—so close to us. So as long as we were small enough to bully, she dragged us to every conceivable meeting the Baptists had—and the Baptists met every night for something. I had learned all the Bible verses and talked with the minister about the scripture and even preached a youth sermon. I was fairly serious about it for a while.

I was about twelve and my glands were acting up. One day I walked over to talk about it with our hewn-from-granite Old Testament preacher and opened without knocking the office door he probably thought he'd locked to find that his and the married choir director's glands were acting up, too—together. To be a little more precise, she was kneeling but I don't think she was praying.

My recollection is that I was only a little surprised and not at all hurt. I remember thinking that it set me free to learn the kinds of sins I could still only dimly imagine—though walking in on them gave me a hint. I think I began to hope that someone would kneel for me that way some day. Maybe it was some sort of classic trauma on a deeper level than I'm aware of, but I remember seeing it at the time as a sign of freedom. I never mentioned it to anyone, but when I told my mother I wasn't interested in church anymore, she didn't argue with me. Maybe she knew more than I realized. Maybe she even knew that disillusionment with people is just the beginning.

I didn't remember Happy's being part of that at all. I told him so.

"Your mother invited me to church," he said in a rather dramatic way. "Do you remember?"

"I'm afraid I don't. Maybe she sensed me slipping away and figured if she could convert both us I'd have a better chance. But I don't remember your ever being there."

"Oh, I came," he said. "One Sunday morning I walked down. I was surprised how much I wanted it. I wasn't even able to tell anybody for years how much I wanted to belong there." He paused.

I was puzzled. "Why didn't you keep coming? Lord

knows they wanted everybody they could get. We had a guy who wore shorty pajamas to church and walked around naked at home with a house full of loose parakeets." I was surprised to hear myself use "Lord knows."

"For one thing, you made fun of it," he said. "You laughed at what they were doing and said you were breaking out as soon as you could."

I stayed quiet.

"For another thing, a woman whispered about my hair."

This was important to him, although I couldn't understand it. His voice carried emotion from all those years ago. "What was wrong with your hair?" I asked finally.

"My DA. Don't you remember? After I'd sat down I heard a woman behind me say to another woman: 'Look at his greasy hair.' She whispered it but I heard it very well. You were sitting beside me. Didn't you?"

I shook my head, amazed at the power of a housewife's catty whisper to hurt this dangerous stranger over miles and years, and at my ability to sit beside him and know nothing of it. His grievance against organized religion seemed even more trivial than mine. "Who cares what some old neighborhood hag thinks about your hair?" I said, with a kid's cocky voice.

"I guess I did," he said. "I felt I couldn't come back."

I didn't know what to make of any of this. It was totally convincing and also silly, the way emotional truth often is.

"But it was wonderful," Happy said, "because it led me eventually to learn that God does welcome me."

"There's something I don't understand," I said after a pause. "If you wanted an organized church, why didn't that satisfy you? Why are you still doing these pamphlets, is I guess what I'm asking. They just don't seem a very effective kind of . . . way of getting your message across." I wished I hadn't brought it up, but Happy seemed pleased.

"Call it superstition," he said. "The guy I met on the beach that night handed me a pamphlet and I kept it. It was printed by the same people who do ours. They aren't sophisticated. They're not written by theologians or rhetoricians. They're simple minded and simplistic sometimes, but I remembered that when I was hurting that's what reached me. Not just the message but the courage of the man to walk up and talk to me and give it to me, and the feeling I had that he cared enough to take that risk, to face that rejection. The people who really need help aren't standing in suits outside Episcopal churches. You find them wandering in a daze like me in dark and dangerous places. The message has to leap out and grab them. I couldn't have gone home and read a chapter from Tielhard or St. Augustine, but I did read the thing he handed me. So that's how we've done it."

I looked at Leila. This had to be one of the stranger evenings in her life. But she wasn't pale and wild eyed and scrunched in her chair like the classic preacher's victim; she seemed animated, fascinated. I had the feeling that she wanted to ask questions, take notes.

She probably would have if Rebecca hadn't hurried into the room carrying a piece of white, lined notebook paper. "Chris left this note in my Bible," she said. "He knows I read it every night. He's run away."

Seventeen

"Not again," Happy said. He lowered his head, closed his eyes and hands and struck his fists together gently in an unconscious gesture of frustration. "We had an understanding. I don't believe it."

"Listen," Rebecca said. "The note's written to you: 'Dear Dad, This isn't like before. This is important. I think you'd agree it's God's work, but I couldn't tell you about it. It's something I must do on my own. Like a miracle, Jennifer came with the money. Pray for me.'"

"Who's Jennifer?" Happy asked.

Rebecca shrugged. Martha shrugged. Leila shrugged. I had a sudden, sinking feeling that I knew who Jennifer might be. "When's the last time he was here?" I asked.

Martha looked at Happy. Happy hesitated. "Yesterday," Rebecca said. "I know he was here when I went to work around four. Martha and I ran the station that afternoon and Dad went to Redding to visit the mission. Chris said he had homework and he was scheduled to work that night."

"He didn't come to relieve us," Martha said. "And when Happy got home he was gone."

"But we thought it was just something . . . that came up," Happy said. "A friend needed help. Something . . . ."

"But who is Jennifer?" Rebecca asked.

"May I use a phone?" I asked.

Sarah was hysterical. "I didn't know how to reach you," she said. "I was about to call Happy's. I don't know what to do. Jennifer's gone again."

"Could she be with her friends again?" I asked, knowing better.

"No, Jesus, listen to this." For a generation that was supposed to be postliterate, it was producing a lot of *billets-doux*. I listened to the phone hit against the table leg several times before Sarah picked it up, out of breath, rustling paper. "Dear Mom, This isn't like before. Finally I have a chance to help someone. Maybe we'll both find out if I have a heart."

"Is her car there?"

"It's at Tampa International. I remembered the name of your friend at the sheriff's office and he checked for me. She flew to San Francisco two days ago and rented a car."

"How's she paying for it?"

Sarah's voice rose. "She's taken her money out of savings and checking—money from relatives, birthdays and such. It added up. She cashed in her gift bonds. She pawned her jewelry. *Hocked* it! And she has a Visa, an American Express, and two gas credit cards. I'm surprised she didn't sell the car to somebody at the airport for a couple hundred bucks, but it was in my name and maybe she didn't have time to find somebody who'd buy it without a title."

"Try to stay calm," I said. I could hear my words echo the way they do when you're offering hollow, automatic comfort. I glanced around the room and saw that nobody there was much consoled, either. And they were really confused. Actually, I didn't have a very clear picture myself, except that Chris and Jennifer seemed to have gotten together for what looked like big-time, high-budget trouble. The Foxes didn't even know yet how much trouble that was likely to be. They didn't even know who Jennifer was, let alone suspect, as I did, how bad it could be with her playing Mother Theresa on Mommy's money.

"I'll call you back as soon as I know more," I said. "I'm at Happy's now. I have a feeling Jennifer and his son, Chris, hooked up. I'll be working on it full time."

"I'm so scared!" Sarah wailed.

"So are we," I said. "But let me go to work. I'll call you tomorrow."

"Tomorrow, hell, call me tonight!"

"It must be after midnight there already."

"You think I can sleep?"

"All right. Let me talk with them and I'll call you back within an hour."

"Spare no expenses. If you have to hire troops, or tanks, hire them. But do it fast. I don't think I can stand much more of this."

"You can stand a lot more than you think. All of us can." I was pretty sure I believed that, or at least that I needed for her to believe it. "I'll call you back, soon."

"When you do, let me talk with Happy."

"Sure."

I hung up and turned to them. "Has Chris had any drug involvement?"

Happy looked at Martha, who didn't seem to offer him a way out. "He spent twenty-eight days in rehab after the last runaway. They had him come back for twenty-eight more. It was summer, so he didn't miss much school. It was this summer. I mean he's just been home a few weeks. He was different. I was sure he was changed."

"He's a lot like you were," Martha said, and Happy looked desperate.

"Let's hope that's not true," I said, hoping for a laugh.

"This is hairy enough."

I got a short one from Leila and a smile, finally, from Happy. "We get it back, don't we?" he asked.

"Hindus call it karma," Leila said.

"I call it the risks of living in the modern world," I said. "Never mind guilt and superstition, although we should recognize again that logic won't be much use here. We got two missing teenagers and the first priority is to get them back. I do that for a living. I gotta level with you now. Sarah hired me to come out here and make sure you were all right. We both felt guilty about not being there when you needed somebody more than Petey, Aldo and Junior."

"You're a private eye?" Happy asked. There was a nice little glow on top of his anxiety now. It's easier to do hard things if you feel that.

"That's the phrase we're stuck with, I guess. Most of my work is in finding runaways. I ought to be able to do this, and I think it needs to be done fast. With the kind of money Jennifer brought out here, they could buy into a lot of grief."

"How did she know Chris?" Rebecca asked. "He never mentioned it."

"My guess is she copied the number from a note her mom made when I called her, then called and got him by accident. Maybe she was just trying to embarrass me or Sarah. Or maybe she asked for him in particular. I think her idea was to prove to us that she wasn't a selfish little rich girl. Sarah and I were a little hard on her, implied she was spoiled, couldn't care about real people in a grown-up way. She's had plenty of recovery and other therapy, which is a kind of boot camp for caring and sharing and all that coded babbleonian vocabulary. She'll show us she can care. Chris is himself recovering. A few words is all it takes to establish rapport between them. She must have struck a chord in Chris. He must have told her the trouble he couldn't tell you, or felt that a stranger could help in ways you couldn't. Sometimes that's the way kids' minds work: Nobody understands me but this other lost street kid. Chris has a problem. Never mind the old folks. Let's show them what *we* can do. Somehow they must have planned it over the phone before she flew out."

"Planned what?" Martha asked.

"I don't have any idea."

We sat in silence for a while. Then Happy said: "Where do we start?"

I knew how to do this. "I want a list of his friends. Good ones and bad ones. Becky, he seemed to trust you. Did he tell you anything?"

Rebecca seemed surprised to hear the short form of her name, but I was a little tired of all these Biblical formalities and I wanted to surprise her anyway.

"No," she said. "I'd tell you. I swear I would." I believed her. Her face was flushed and she was very beautiful.

Leila noticed me noticing. "Well, now," Leila said, "how can *I* help."

"You stand by," I said, grinning in what I hoped was a disarming way. "Becky, you make the list. What day is this?"

"Friday," Martha said.

"Good. I can see some kids tomorrow. It's not too late for me to make some calls tonight. I also need to reach the director of that rehab place. Is it nearby?"

"Up near Mount Shasta," Happy said. "We won't open the station tomorrow."

"My experience tells me that might be a bad idea," I said. "I think you'd all be better off working tomorrow. It'll keep you busy and give me some freedom to move around. I'll know where to reach you. Worried parents can be a real obstacle. Maybe you could close down at five and we'll buy some chicken buckets and see where our strategy has gotten us."

"Will you need my help?" Becky asked. "They don't need me at the station. I could help explain the kids."

"No, thanks," I said, smiling. "I've got Leila."

"You'll send me a bill," Happy said.

"Fat chance," I said. "Sarah's paying expenses and I'm donating my time."

"How will you approach his friends?" Happy asked.

"I think I'm a *Rolling Stone* reporter who wants to interview Chris as a teenage Christian black belt."

"Would they do that?" Becky asked.

"Sure. And even if they wouldn't, the kids will believe it. It's what they live for. Becky, please make me two lists—druggie friends and churchy friends."

Leila cleared her throat. Was I being insensitive, assuming Chris had no friends in what we all hoped was still the majority between the extremes? Nobody else seemed to have noticed.

While Becky worked on the list, I called Sarah on the kitchen phone. I asked her to call Romanello at home tonight and get him to find out if anyone had called Happy's number from hers. That would give us a solid connection between Jennifer and Chris. I didn't think Jennifer was the type to take a pocket full of change to a phone booth. Then I put Happy on with a warning that it was getting late and I had calls to make, and to give him some room I asked Martha to show me Chris's room again. Leila went with us. I looked for hiding places, diaries, notes in favorite books. I found nothing. It looked like the room of a kid who'd gone away to college or the service.

I returned to the kitchen and signalled Happy it was time to sign off. "God bless you," he said, and handed me the receiver.

"He's wonderful," Sarah said. "I feel so much better."

"Good," I said. "Now call Romanello before he goes to bed. He probably won't be able to get on it until tomorrow. Call us here when you get an answer."

"God bless you," Sarah said. She did sound better.

"Not you, too," I said.

"No atheists in foxholes," she said.

"Whatever works," I said, and we hung up.

I called the rehab place, a private hospital, and told the duty counselor I had an emergency and needed to talk with the director as soon as possible. The woman said the director was rock-hounding that weekend, but if he checked in they would ask him to call me. I went to work on the list, which Becky said included seven friends—three of them still druggies and therefore off limits to Happy, and four of them from church. No girlfriend, not since he got back from rehab. Old girlfriend? One from the year before, a real party pal, but she'd moved with her parents to L.A.

Only one of the numbers didn't answer, and with all three druggie kids I got parents. One said her son was out for the evening. The second said her son was missing. The third said her son was dead. She didn't say how; I didn't ask. It sounded recent. I said I was sorry. I gave the *Rolling Stone* story and made an appointment to meet the druggie kid who was out at noon the next day. His mother said he didn't get up much before that.

Of the straight kids whose numbers answered, only one was not home, and I made appointments for earlier in the day. "You're going to waste a lot of time finding those addresses," Becky said, looking to Leila instead of me. "I could save you a lot of work."

"Becky should come with us," Leila said, and reached out to hug her.

"We'll come by at eight," I said. "I'll try this remaining no-answer later tonight and tomorrow morning."

"Let me see that," Martha said. She peered at the list in that worried way. "I know where that family is," she said. "They're at a weekend retreat and probably won't be back till Sunday night."

"Thanks," I said. "Call us at the motel if anything comes up." We began moving toward the door. Leila gave me a funny look. When it was clear I didn't understand, she turned to Happy and Martha and said: "We're registered as Mr. and Mrs. Joseph Smith."

Eighteen

To an observer like Leila, the first of my Saturday interviews were a waste of my limited acting ability, not to mention my time. But that's how an investigation is done. You approach the truth of what happened very slowly, often by process of elimination. Everybody I talked with wanted to be in *Rolling Stone*—including the born-againers and their parents—but nobody knew where Chris was. I've done this so long that I can usually smell a liar.

I spent the early morning in neat living rooms and Spartan bedrooms, where several parents and one kid tried to sell me Jesus—assuming from my appearance and profession, I guess, that I didn't already have some. Leila and Becky stayed in the car, to keep my *Rolling Stone* cover in place. Where there was a chance Becky would be seen, they parked around a corner and I walked up.

I visited the parents of the missing druggie friend, who tried to hire me to find him. He'd been missing for three weeks, but it was his second runaway. They'd been through everything with the police and done everything short of hiring a PI and putting his picture on milk cartons. He was a little too old for milk cartons, and I already had a case. Two cases, maybe, although I hoped they were the same. Nobody had heard of a girl named Jennifer, which surprised me since the US was crawling with them, along with Tracys and Stacys and Seans and Brians. These parents lived in a well-tended split-level in an upscale neighborhood. Both were teachers, and they seemed sober and sincere people, the kind of folks who gave the kid everything a kid could want, including love and attention, and watched him turn despite it—overnight, they always said—into a sociopathic stranger.

Here was where all the theories seemed to break down. I never knew what to tell them. You could do it all right and still lose the kid. You could do it all wrong and the kid would rise above it. Was it environment or was it heredity or was it just drugs? Some of us seemed predisposed to love drugs, to grasp them early and hold them close in a world we never made. It wasn't a very nice world. It wasn't honest, or smart, or kind most of the time. To an adolescent, it seemed even worse because disillusionment was new. With drugs it could be handled. Instead of growing up you could play a role, with appropriate drugs, costumes, soundtrack. Some on my list substituted religion.

Happy and I drank our first beers together. We were fifteen. Mine was a classic Ozzie and Harriet home; his was the classic broken, alcoholic home; for both of us it was a taste of God. I remember it vividly. We got one of the denizens of the 4010 Club to bring us out a cold six-pack of Busch Bavarian, as it was then called. We paid him, covered it with Happy's jacket, and ran down the alley to a vacant lot with a clump of tall palmettos that would shield us. The cans were beaded with condensed Florida humidity, exotic in shape and color, magic in their potential.

No church key! I ran to the hardware store, pale and shaking. It was closed. I tried the greasy Greek at the corner drive-in. He frowned and nodded knowingly, but he gave me one. When I got back we cracked two beers and looked at each other and laughed. Then we drank a sip, looked at each other again with revelation dawning, and drank half our cans. I can still remember how it was cold and warm at once, how it filled a void in me I didn't know was there. We looked at each other like thieves in a vault of diamonds. "Jesus," Happy said. "Damn," I replied. Then we drank the remaining four beers in a hurry and got another six-pack and a pack of Viceroys. We had ourselves an evening.

Happy got caught coming in. I guess his mother knew the signs better. Maybe she'd been expecting it. But she didn't call mine, who was in bed early and missed me. I lay in bed that night with an oceanic feeling, dreaming of Attila, Genghis, Tamerlane, Alexander the Great, Suleiman the Magnificent.

By coincidence, I suppose, I had my last bar drink in the 4010 Club, which had been done over as an East Side New York fern bar and had a real New York bartender whom I'd known on the West Side. He shut me off—the first and last time in my life, I hope. I couldn't believe it. I had a noseful of crystal methedrine and knew I couldn't be drunk. He insisted. I was deeply hurt and gave up drinking in bars, but it was a while before I gave it up altogether, a very long, low, sad while.

I told the teacher parents how sorry I was and went to my last appointment, a far funkier house that stirred up more of my old ghosts. It was the home of the only live and resident druggie former friend of Chris Fox. His mother opened the door. I knew where the kid was from the paint-peeling heavy metal concert. I could have found the house from several blocks away. The mother wore a Tom Petty and the Heartbreakers concert-tour T-shirt over her nipples, which were reminiscent in shape and color of the bar sausages they used to sell at Dottie's. She watched my eyes watching her nipples and smiled. I wondered when both of us would get tired of doing this. Her breasts were tiring, and her liver was ruining her waistline. The house smelled like the Grateful Dead's laundry hamper. "You're from *Rolling Stone*," she said. "I'm Fay. We have a subscription."

I'd seen this story all over the country. She'd given the kid freedom. A joint for his twelfth birthday, maybe, casual maternal nudity so he didn't grow up ignorant of the female anatomy, a succession of mellow dudes for role models and bonding, and no hassle about picking up his room. The house was a health risk. The freedom of the damned. One day Little League, the next day full-bore Bohemia, whether he wanted it or not. Kidnapped by Hipness. Maybe what the kid wants most is a clean house and a mother who wears a bra. But he can't have that so he decorates his little corner of hell according to his own taste. Fay went to get Brian. Either she'd cut off her jeans in 1974 or she'd lost touch with what a sober man wanted to see.

Brian turned off the stereo and came out. I was grateful. I had a feeling the living room was as much as I wanted to see of this place. He was a skinny, jumpy kid who seemed to be losing some of his hair already. Fay stayed with us. We talked. We got nowhere. He wasn't a fan of Christian karate. Suddenly he said: "Chris's parents ruined him. That's the real story. They sent him to that concentration camp, made him pass out those stupid pamphlets, hang out with those geeks." His words had the flavor of one of those coerced hostage statements.

"I heard he ran away," I said. "Couldn't hack it any more."

"You have to give a child some space," Fay said smugly, like somebody on the Donahue show.

"I'm curious. I came down to do this piece and I find

out he's split again. Maybe he went back to wherever he was before. Maybe that's a better story, but I got a deadline on this piece. Maybe I could talk with him there. It isn't gonna work if I can't find him."

Brian seemed genuinely frustrated. Agitated would be a better word. "I wish I could," he said. "He wouldn't talk with us after they sent him away. Alls I know is that before they sent him away he was someplace in the hills. There's a commune up there in the dope county—a tribe, he said, when he first got back. Jeff went with him."

"Is that the missing kid?"

"Yeah, missing, right," he said sarcastically. "Like a turkey wants to be missing at Thanksgiving."

Brian's metaphor surprised me. "So he had it tough?" I asked, thinking of the two worried teachers.

"You should meet his parents," Brian said. "Leave it to Beaver."

"You think Chris and Jeff went back to this place?"

I didn't tell Brian that Jeff and Chris had left at different times, or about Jennifer. Brian's interest and energy seemed to come in spurts, alternating with periods of apathy. "I dunno," he said dully. "Maybe."

"Tell me more about it." I said. "I've heard stories about such places. This could be a better story than I thought."

Brian gave my encouragement a few beats to kick in, like a drug. "People live in tents and yurts and these Indian-type houses. I can't remember what they're called, but they make 'em out of mud and wood and they're dug into the ground. They grow dope—sinsemilla. You can stay high. You got girls and music. You sell the dope. All you got to do is take care of the crop and make sure you don't get ripped off."

He made it sound like El Dorado. "Why don't you go?" I asked.

Brian hesitated. Even if he knew where it was, he

wouldn't go anywhere. Mom had brought it all home. He lacked the desperation that made explorers and adventurers. Even Cortez burned his ships to motivate his men. "He never got to tell us where it was," he said finally. "They made him stay away from us. We were a bad influence. Jeff's parents tried to do the same thing. Shit. We were gonna go visit, but they put them away like some Gestapo thing." Brian looked for approval at his mother, and got it.

"You don't need people like that," Fay said, a weird twist on parental advice.

Brian needed somebody besides Mom, but that wasn't my case. Maybe he'd be one of those bizarre kids who turned their parents in. More likely, you could find Fay and Brian right here ten years from now, digging a deeper groove.

I said good-bye to Fay and Brian. As I rounded the corner to the car, I heard his Metallica crank up again and wondered why the neighbors put up with it. Everybody seemed to be conspiring to give Brian more freedom than he knew what to do with. It seemed that Chris had stayed away from Brian and his other druggie friends. And maybe he couldn't tell his approved friends what was eating him. But unless he was one in a million, he had to tell somebody. Most of us do. If Becky was telling the truth—and I believed she was—then he didn't tell her, and it had to be somebody in rehab. I'd been through enough drug and alcohol treatments to know that if they're any good at all, that's where you talk about your life.

We went home and had lunch. Sarah called to say that Romanello had checked with the phone company and yes, Jennifer had called Happy's number. I called the rehab and got a different duty counselor who said that the director might check in that evening. It was a guy this time and he wasn't encouraging. I decided to level with him.

"I'm representing the parents of Chris Fox. Do you know him?"

"Very well. What's happened?"

"Chris is gone again."

"Oh, no," the guy said. His disappointment sounded genuine. "He was one I thought we wouldn't lose."

"I think there's more going on here than recidivism," I said, hoping, I suppose, to impress him with some professional jargon. As a frequent recidivist, I'd come by the word the hard way. "I have a feeling that his motives are unselfish, that he hopes to rescue somebody, but it's very dangerous for him."

"And you want to know where he went?" Suddenly the man's voice seemed farther away. Maybe it dawned on both of us just how many places people could go to disappear.

"Yes. I think he's been there before and there's unfinished business. Nobody here knows. I hoped he might have told somebody in treatment."

"That's confidential. I mean he never told me, but all of this is confidential."

"I know. I've been there."

"Here?" he said, misunderstanding.

I told him where, from the places with tennis courts and swimming pools to the VA and the county detox.

"You're recovering?"

"A day at a time," I said, offering a little pious signal.

He paused. "I still can't help you." He paused again. "Without permission."

"How about I drive up there and when the director gets back we'll ask him?"

"Fine."

"I'll bring my license and ask the Foxes to call you with their permission."

"I can't promise," he said. I knew that. He gave me directions. I called the station and asked Happy to call him right away. I told him Leila and I might not be back for supper, but to save us some chicken.

Nineteen

Leila and I found the treatment center about three. If you're going someplace to sweat and fidget and hyperventilate and throw up and have hallucinations and convulsions and learn to live a desperate breath at a time, you might as well do it with Mount Shasta rising above you. Under the inactive volcano.

A guy pulled up after us in a Jeep with a canvas top. He was sunburned, built like a badger and wearing khaki shorts, boots, a white T-shirt, a canvas hat, and a goatee. It has been my experience that guys with goatees usually turn out to be either shrinks or pornographers, so I figured here was our director. But we played the silly game of not knowing who we were. I found the reception desk and the counselor named Dan—a guy around thirty with curly black hair and beard and some very well-worn overalls—while the guy in shorts went around back to his own entrance and emerged from his office after a while to shake my hand. "Welcome to the Shasta Center," he said. "I'm Syd Ringer."

"Dr. Ringer. My colleague, Leila Sweeting." Ringer smiled very big. Leila could guarantee that. "The location reminds me of *Under the Volcano*," I said.

He understood my allusion to Lowry's great alcoholic

novel and laughed appreciatively. "I thought of calling the place *Out From Under the Volcano*," he said.

"Advertise in *The New Yorker*," I said, and we laughed. Leila gave me a look which said, You're getting silly and blowing this interview. She was probably right.

"Please come in," Ringer said. "Dan, would you join us?" We found chairs. His degrees were on the wall and his family on the desk. "Dan told me something about your problem on the phone," he said, his T-shirt and canvas hat out of place in the leather executive chair. He lit a Salem. "How can I help?"

"I think Chris and the daughter of a friend of mine from Florida have gone up into the dope country on some kind of rescue mission. They took a lot of money. Maybe they hope to buy somebody's freedom. I think they're in a lot of trouble. I need to find somebody that Chris may have confided in. I've already talked with all his friends. I thought maybe here in treatment."

"Dan tells me you've been through treatment yourself."

"Yes. I understand how important confidentiality is. I'm asking you to weigh that against the probability that Chris and Jennifer have gone up into the dope country with a lot of cash and very little sense of their real danger."

"I hope they're not going to buy dope," Ringer said.

"The harvest should be over by now," Dan said.

"Of course. It would be," Ringer said. "It's been so dry, they'd have harvested what they could before they lost it all." He turned to Dan. "Do we know anything about this?"

"I made some calls to the other counselors," Dan said. "Chris mentioned the trip in therapy and individual sessions . . ." Dan paused, wondering if he'd gone too far. Ringer made a motion for him to continue. ". . . but he didn't mention anyone in trouble, anyone that he'd left behind. He wasn't specific about where the place was. To the southwest of here was my impression, over in the mountains. Redwood County, maybe. He didn't seem too worried about it."

"My guess is he felt an obligation to handle it himself," I said. "He would have avoided it in therapy."

"I think he was serious about getting well," Dan said, a little indignant. Ringer nodded.

I nodded. "Everything points to that. I've been talking all morning to people who knew him. He seems to have avoided his old friends. He made some new ones. But this was eating at him. It may have something to do with his friend, Jeff, who went there with him the first time. At least I think they were together. I'm not sure when Jeff got home from that first runaway, but maybe when he couldn't get along at home he just went back. I think he and Chris were under orders to avoid each other. Maybe Chris felt responsible."

Leila saw I needed something and reached out to me for my notebook. She went to call Jeff's parents. I was embarrassed to have missed that but grateful she hadn't.

Ringer gave Dan a questioning look. Dan gave Ringer a shrug. I felt we were right on the edge of an executive decision. "Is Jeremy here tonight?" Ringer asked.

Dan nodded. "He didn't want weekend leave."

Ringer shook his head sadly and turned back to me. I could hear Leila on the phone. "Let's wait for your colleague," Ringer said. "In the meantime, let me just confirm your credentials. Dan says Mr. Fox called."

I showed him my wallet ID and offered to let him call Sarah. He declined. Leila joined us and Ringer waited for her report.

"Jeff came back the same time Chris did," she said. "But he would never admit to his parents that he and Chris went to the same place. Actually, his parents said, he's been gone almost a month this time."

"Chris was in treatment here then," Dan said.

"So he found out when he got home," I said. "He stayed away from his other party pals, but maybe he felt an obligation to Jeff."

"Go see Jeremy," Ringer said to Dan. "Explain the circumstances. Ask if he'll talk to Mr. Sierra. I want you to be there, too." Dan left.

"Jeremy isn't very trusting of women," Ringer said. "His mother has finally invited him home for a weekend after more than ninety days here, and he refused to go."

"Ninety days?" Leila asked.

"Jeremy's a harder case than most. Maybe you'd let me show you around the place, if Jeremy agrees to see them."

"Charmed," Leila said, "but I'd think you could even get a guy to trust women in ninety days."

"It takes us a long time to get sick," Ringer said. "Sometimes the cure takes at least as long. We've ended up doing more and more work with drug-addicted and cross-addicted young people than with older alcoholics. We didn't plan to do it, but that seemed to be the greatest need. The irony is that sometimes it seems harder to change a kid who's only had his habit for a few months than the classic, low-bottom, thirty-year alcoholic. And when you mix drugs, the way most folks do these days, you complicate the issue. You know all about that, Mr. Sierra."

"I hope I know enough," I said.

"Why don't we start the tour," he said. "We'll wander down that way and Dan will see us." He rose and ushered us out his back door. The place seemed to have been built around an older motel. Everything that hadn't been made of redwood was now covered with it. We'd just come from the original office, which had been expanded for more office and meeting space. Three wings of motel-like rooms spread in a fanlike pattern from it back into the pines. This was a minimum security situation, even if they wanted it otherwise.

"Our clients stay in the rooms. Everybody has a roommate. Jeremy was Chris's. Frankly, Jeremy's a very difficult young man, and Chris seemed best able to cope with him—maybe even help him as a friend. I think they got pretty close." He stubbed out his cigarette in the gravel, then picked it up and carried it as we walked along. "We've had our consciousness raised a little here, about tobacco and coffee and other over-the-counter drugs. We found out, for example, that it's physically and mentally much easier to quit everything at once. I haven't been able to quit this yet, but I have learned not to throw them around." He lifted the top of a large coyote- and raccoon-proof trash can and tossed in the butt.

"I'm glad to hear that," I said. "In the early days I think they thought caffeine, nicotine, and sugar were the cure for drugs and booze. I think I've stayed sober so I didn't have to sit around any more smoky rooms."

"We're living in the dark ages," Ringer said. "We don't even know how to use the knowledge we *do* have. They're going to be as puzzled by us in the future—assuming there is one—as we are by cannibalism, foot-binding, or clitorectomies. It's all a shot in the dark, but we do what we can."

I liked Ringer. He showed us a new building with NO SMOKING signs on all the doors. It housed the kitchen and dining area, and a television lounge on the main floor and a gym in the basement, with a whirlpool and steambath. "We try everything," he said as we wandered through. "We have a massage therapist from nearby and an acupuncturist on call. What the hell, it can't hurt." He was lighting another Salem outside when Dan found us.

"He'll talk with you," Dan told me, "but he's not in a good mood."

* * *

It was hard to believe that Jeremy had ever been in a good mood. Or that the sun had ever touched his subterranean pallor. There were holes around the periphery of his ears where I guessed safety pins had lived, and a hole in his nostril for an absent diamond. There was some darkening fuzz on his cheeks and neck, probably just at the cusp of what the counselors would decide was a mature beard and make him shave. His hair was cut very close to the scalp with clippers—probably the only cure for the haircut he came in with. Apparently he had decided to keep it that way. His body was elongated and pale, like a movie alien. He seemed remarkably long waisted. He had the huge, pupil-filled eyes and long, damp, delicate fingers of a lemur or other night creature. He was wearing faded jeans and a very incongruous light-blue Izod polo shirt.

Dan had explained on the way that the staff made no concessions to strange dress or makeup or hairstyles—which were viewed as part of the behavioral problem. You had a choice of a straight haircut or no hair at all. If you stayed straight long enough you could get to be a counselor and wear a beard and overalls. Jeremy was wearing unlaced sneakers which I guessed Dan had told him to put on for my visit. All the barbers, tailors, wiggers, and makeup wizards in Hollywood couldn't make Jeremy look normal. Couldn't even get him into the ballpark. He sat in a tan armchair staring at a blank TV screen.

"This is Mr. Sierra," Dan said.

Jeremy waited. I waited with him. I had friends like this, too. "Chris is in trouble," I said after a while.

He turned to look at me. He reminded me of a caged animal, one that wouldn't run even if you threw open all the doors and fired cannon. "Did he go back there?" he asked. His voice was gentle for a guy who'd worn safety pins in his ears.

"I think so. But I won't know unless I can find it. I think he needs help getting out."

Jeremy understood that. He moved a little in the tan chair and began a kind of chant, like the Aztec memorizers who carried messages they never understood:

"South on I-5. West on state road 295 for a long way. Stay on that until you get to Darbyville. Begin counting miles at the Broken Wheel Restaurant and keep driving west out of town. Drive thirty-seven-and-three-tenths miles from the Broken Wheel and turn right on a paved road. That road winds around and crosses two bridges. Once it forks. Take the right fork. It will take you to a small lumber town called Gancy. Keep right on that road and skirt the town to the right or east. Don't drive through the main street. Stay on the road until the pavement ends just north of town. Begin counting miles where the pavement ends. Drive ten-and-four-tenths miles on the dirt road and you will reach an unimproved, one-lane dirt road to the right. Take it about fifteen miles until you reach the lumber company fence. Leave your car there. Follow the lumber company road for about six miles until it ends at the Middle Fork of the Van Horn River. Ford the river. There is a path along the far bank. Take it upstream. After about ten miles you will pass between a flat-topped mountain on the left and a mountain on the right, called Bread Loaf because of its shape. Now you are in the wilderness area.

"Soon you will pass through the people who try to live like the Hoopa. They are mostly good people but guard their crops with rifles and shotguns. They grow dope and vegetables and raise rabbits. They build houses like the Hoopa Indians and stay through the winter. They may welcome you. They may not. They fear outsiders and the bad people beyond. They smoke a lot of dope and don't think like us anymore. If you're going beyond, it might be better to pass unnoticed by the people who live like the

Hoopa. They have sentries during the harvest time and post lookouts at other times for the bad people upstream. Their dogs warn them, too. You will have to find another way than the path.

"The bad people live about four miles beyond the Hoopa. They have some off-road vehicles and bring gas in for them. They have built some yurts and shacks, and some live inside the mine shaft underneath the twin-peaked mountain called Devil's Horns. Their village is just outside the mine shaft, about a half-mile up a path from the river. If you follow the river path you will see it, but they will see you. They have sentries and guns and dogs. In the harvest time they have booby traps. Sometimes they raid the Hoopa people for food and to try to fuck their women."

Jeremy stopped. I was scribbling to catch up. I had the feeling that if I asked him for details or elaboration he would start over, at the beginning. "Have you ever been there?" I asked.

He shook his head. He had remembered it all from Chris's telling. I had a feeling that Jeremy couldn't read or write. It seemed to be true of many of the drug-damaged kids I'd found and brought back. Like pre-literate man, he was compensating.

"Is there anything else?"

Something came to him. "The bad ones call themselves the Midnight Mine Folk. They don't want to spend the winter there," he said. "The winters are very hard there. This year wasn't such a good crop. They need more money to go south."

"Don't we all," I said. He smiled, or maybe I just imagined it. "Maybe they've got reservations in Acapulco." I didn't get another smile.

Then Jeremy said, in the same monotone: "Also, they're trying to learn to cook speed to make more money. In the cave, probably. The bikers will buy and distribute it and it's easier to get out than grass. If they're doing that you can follow the smell because it smells like urine."

"Thank you, Jeremy," I said. "I'll do my best to help Chris. You've done more good than you know."

He didn't say anything. I indicated with my eyes to Dan that I was leaving. He nodded. Outside, I realized that I'd dropped my pen on the carpet. I went back. It was the only pen I had. Dan was leaning toward Jeremy. Jeremy hadn't moved. His pale face was still blank, and washed with tears.

Twenty

Doc Ringer spread several maps across the top of his desk. Lucky for us he was an outdoor guy. We started with a triple-A map to get the general picture, then switched to a Metzker's map of Redwood County and finally a Forest Service map which included the wilderness area and gave us a better topographical picture. The directions made sense. We found the river, the Flattop and Bread Loaf Mountains, the Devil's Horns Mountain, and the Midnight Mine. They were given official names on the map. "Take 'em," Ringer said. "I don't need 'em." I marked our way and folded them. "Let us know what happens," he said.

I asked him if I could use the phone and he said sure. I asked him what was the Redwood County seat and he said Fremont. I got the sheriff's office number from information and made a credit-card call to it.

I got a busy signal for a long time and finally asked the operator to put me through on their emergency number. I got a breathless deputy and asked him if I had a wrong number before. I told him the line kept ringing busy.

"You don't listen to the news," he said. "The sheriff's been shot and a deputy killed. There's only two of us here. If this ain't the end of the world, you better call back tomorrow. I got to clear this emergency line."

I told Ringer about it and he took us over to the TV lounge. There were two clients there, watching a game show. Ringer asked if we could switch to the news. Somebody had ambushed the sheriff and two of his deputies in the southern part of the county. One deputy was dead and the sheriff was in critical condition. Deputies wanted blood. It was dope growers, one said. The sheriff's party had been in civilian clothes, in an unmarked car, looking for evidence of some late harvesting. They had with them a representative of the governor, who wanted to crack down on dope growers. There'd been a lot of resistance because it was also the highest yielding crop in the history of California agriculture. The sheriff must have known the harvest was in and probably figured this for a P.R. tour, a milk run. Somebody had fired on the car with an automatic weapon.

Every spare policeman for five counties around was gathering to surround and sweep the southern county. The Highway Patrol had sealed it off. It was a long county. The north, where we needed to go, was miles away.

"It doesn't look good," I said.

"But they're motivated," Leila said. "Once they round up those creeps, we can send 'em up north for ours. They're in a posse state of mind."

"I read that violent crime has gone up a hundred-and-fifty percent a year in some of those dope-growing counties," said Ringer. "Maybe this'll be where they draw the line."

"All of that may be true," I said, "but the last thing we want near our people is an angry posse. We want them out alive, and it has to happen fast. Every day the situation gets worse. These aren't even your typical kidnappers."

"We're not sure they're there," Leila said.

"Right," I admitted. "We need to do that first."

"What about the FBI?" Ringer asked.

"I'll get right on it," I lied. Leila and I already had a good idea how they worked, and how much they wanted to help me. Ringer wanted me to call them right then, but I told him I had a special number in my gear back at the Foxes's, and I'd call them tonight.

We said goodbye and hit the road. Then I stopped at the first phone booth and made the call I needed to make, which was to the SEAL Team in Coronado. "Seaman Canady speaking on a non-secure phone," a voice answered. The watch messenger, a hot dog just out of BUDS who still planned on kicking the world's ass. I told him I'd been on the Team and was looking for some old friends. He didn't feel friendly. He told me to put an ad in *Navy Times*.

"You're stepping on your crank, Canady. If I have to come there to find my running mates you're going to have a major change of heart, and face."

Canady had his change of heart right there and gave me the OOD, a chief named Bomonti. "Who you looking for?" Bomonti asked.

"Give me some names, please, Chief. First classes and above."

"How about you give me some names first. We got security concerns here." I gave him names of guys I was with in BUDS. He stopped me when I came to Fred Bone. "Chief Bone's with us here," he said. "Hold on, I'll ask around." It shouldn't have surprised me that Bone was already a chief. A lot of time had passed. I waited for some more time and a few more trucks to go by. Then I heard a different voice.

"Bone speaking."

"You on duty?"

"Not exactly. Who's this?"

"Sierra."

"I'll be dipped in shit. Let me call you back on a secure phone. What's your number?"

I gave it to him, and told him it was a phone booth in the middle of nowhere.

"OK," Bone said. "Your end's clean. Let's sanitize mine. Give me five to ten."

At almost seven, the phone rang. "Where are you, sleeve?"

"Northern California."

"And you just missed me?"

"Are you on duty or not?"

"No, I was just passing through. Checked in after chow. Got to keep an eye on these pussies."

"You're not married?"

"I *was* married—twice. Fuck that."

"Congratulations."

"Thanks. Why don't you come down?"

"I'm doing private security work. I got a big problem and need some help."

"You want the whole brotherhood or just an elite few?"

"I wish I could. I gotta do it myself. I need some weapons, special stuff. You know anybody up this way deals hardware?"

"Good friend outside Chico."

"Would you call him for me?"

"You're not gonna do anything freaky."

"How freaky could it be?"

"I'm not sure either of us ever found out how freaky it could be, but if you'd stayed in you'd have a better idea. We've done some weird shit."

"I'm dealing with some very weird people, in a tough place to get into. I need an advantage. These people are mutant hippie dope-growing freaks living up in the mountains."

"Say no more. Wait fifteen minutes and call Buddy

Dykstra. Wait, I got my address book here." He fumbled around and then gave me the number. "If he ain't there I'll keep calling. If you get him first, tell him to call me at the CPO Club."

"Must be nice."

"It's a great life. See the world. Meet interesting people and kill them. Too bad you fucked over your knee. You missed 'Nam. Our guys were the only Grenada casualties. They sent us with too much equipment and some bad skinny on the tides and current. Never even got ashore."

"I heard. I knew Riley and Swanker."

"We had a good party for 'em. We took the first casualties in Panama, too. Now you're gonna miss Niggeragua, or Peru, or another visit to Sodom Hussein."

"Some people have all the luck," I said. Irony wasn't Bone's strong suit. I thanked him and he hung up, probably still feeling sorry for me.

The remaining Foxes had already eaten, but they'd saved us some chicken and Martha heated up some other stuff and poured us iced tea. I gave a modified version of the day's events to the whole group. I stressed the fact that I had no proof of where they'd gone and didn't mention that the whole of law enforcement in this part of California was hunting some cop killers in the wrong end of Redwood County.

Later I took Happy outside into the hot, dry, Indian terrain just beyond his watered lawn—itself in grave danger since the sprinkling ban—and told him the real story.

"What can we do?" he asked. I couldn't see him very well out there. His voice sounded steady and neutral. Maybe he had an idea what was coming.

"Like old times, " I said. "We're going to have to kick some ass."

Twenty-one

The Fox women ran the station and Happy, Leila, and I left early the next morning. We followed the map. Just before Darbyville we passed a sign for a macrobiotic summer camp. Ahh, California. A taste of everything in the human heart. "We can't kill anybody," Happy said after we'd turned onto the first dirt road. He'd been thinking about it for miles.

"We'll try not to," I said. "Killing isn't easy to explain. The cops are hunting dopers now, but that doesn't mean we have a license."

"Not that," he said. "Because it's wrong."

"I don't like the idea either."

"You ever kill anybody?" he asked.

"Two men," I said, hoping it would stop there.

"As a SEAL," he said, trying to reassure himself.

"They don't guarantee you a trophy, like some fancy hunting lodge. I blew my knee in jump school at Benning. I killed two guys in Atlanta because they'd thrown me into a trunk and planned to kill me. Did it with a tire iron."

Happy did not seem reassured.

"So how do you know how to do this?" Leila asked, even less reassured.

"Geez," I said. "I know a *few* things. The rest I'll have to figure out as we go along. If I get in too deep we'll call Rambo."

"You know there's not a goddamn thing funny about this," Leila said. It was nice having somebody worry about me. We rode slowly through Gancy, a tiny lumber-mill town with a couple of parked trucks and a few dusty kids staring at us as we passed. This wasn't on anybody's way to anywhere, and any visitors probably deserved a certain amount of suspicion. I was looking for the rental car. We found the dirt road and then the logging road and drove to where the fence blocked it, where we found a Hertz-owned little Dodge. I wrote down its tag number. The kids had locked it. We decided to leave it in case they made a break and were counting on having it there.

Happy adjusted to the truth. By the time we got back to Darbyville, he was ready to do it. I called the agency and confirmed Jennifer as the renter of that car. I called Dykstra and arranged a meet. I asked him if he needed cash and he said that if we agreed on a price, Sarah could wire him the money and he'd arrange a delivery. It was probably safer for him to have the two things happen at different times. I called Sarah, gave her a quick rundown, and asked her to take out ten grand just in case and be ready to wire some of it. I told her it was up to her and Happy whether to wait for a ransom demand or act now. I could deliver the money, if these Manson strikers ever thought of asking for it. I told her I wasn't sure they were straight enough to know how to use the phone anymore. She didn't have to think it over.

I told her not to answer her phone, but to go to a friend's and stay where I could reach her. If they couldn't reach her at home, it would buy us more time. She gave me a friend's number. She wanted to fly out and join us, but I thought we might still need her to answer the phone and stall in Florida. I figured the burnouts would use the phone here in Gancy whenever it dawned on them what to do and they gathered enough small change, but it wasn't smart waiting for them. The kids could already be dead, if Jennifer had chosen this worst of all possible times to pretend her mommy wasn't rich.

I thought about asking in town whether any of the outback people had been in to use the phone, but it might get back to them. We needed to know so much more, and the lay of the land was such that if we were lucky enough to get back there and find out without being seen, we might as well stay and do the job.

Dykstra lived in his shop—an enormous, concrete-block, metal-roofed building in the desert. It had its own inside firing range. He wasn't exactly what I expected. He seemed entirely too chubby and rosy cheeked to be a dangerous gun fanatic, although he was wearing a "Death From Above" Airborne T-shirt. You could tell that he'd had to work a little harder to overcome his cherubic appearance. He'd finally gotten the Hard Look down, and when he did move, he moved knowingly and with a kind of controlled fury. He handled the guns that way, and it made us jumpy.

"I wouldn't presume to advise a friend of Bone's about tactics," he said.

"I might need some advice," I said. "I don't know the country out here."

"Anything I can do," he said.

"Is the deer season still on?"

"The buck season runs a couple more weeks. It ain't much good because it's so dry. Deer don't move around much in this heat. Where you talkin' about?"

"Northeast of here, in the mountains."

He thought about that, obviously wondering if we were part of the hunt for the cop-killers. I let him think what he wanted. "If what you want is a cover, then carrying deer guns is O.K. Actually, there aren't many sporting reasons to be out in those hills now, but this is as good as any. I can sell you a license here, although I doubt there'll be many game people out there in this heat any more than deer. I been half expecting 'em to put a ban on hunting and hiking until the rains come, especially over there in Redwood. They got all they can handle."

"I got that impression," I said.

"These people trained?" he asked of Happy and Leila.

"My old friend here gets a quick course, from you. The lady drops and picks up."

"You realize this is all demo. If you buy, it happens with other merch. We agree on a spot and you pick it up. Except for the conventional stuff, which we can do right now. Need handguns?"

"We're covered. I think one of us should carry a shotgun, the other a good sniper rifle. Need a night scope for it."

"Outstanding. I've been testing a nice little Ultra Light. Under six pounds with an ordinary scope. The one I've got is chambered for .223 Remington. Want something bigger?"

"No. I just want the option of taking somebody out at a distance. I'd rather wound than kill."

"Goes against my principles, but never mind. I can put an image-intensifier scope on it, but since it's illegal to hunt at night it might look suspicious. The scope's pretty big, but you could pack it and put it on later. I've got a first generation starlight right here in the shop—the lightest and cheapest we're going to find and more than adequate for the operation you've described. Adaptable to daylight, too. For a shotgun, I recommend the Remington 870 twelve-gauge with shoulder stock. Gives you five rounds and is a standard deer-hunting weapon. Double- or triple-ought buck. I know you guys liked Ithacas but I don't have one."

"Number six shot is fine," I said.

Dykstra made a face. "O.K., so you're hunting birds. These are what you carry outside. But I have a feeling there's more of a tactical advantage needed here. Something concealable and with a lot of firepower?"

"Uzi, I think. With suppressor and as many extra magazines as we can carry. Suppressor on the rifle, too."

"You tell me, but some of those magazines need to be loaded with subsonic rounds, if you're going to use the suppressor. I'd say maybe eight extra sticks, thirty rounds each, half of them subsonic. There's an Uzi .45 caliber now, too, and a conversion kit to .22. I mean, you're using birdshot, so—"

"The nine-millimeter's fine." I waited a couple of beats to let Dykstra get the grab-ass out of his system. "Can you help us rig it behind his backpack with velcro straps or hooks, so I can snatch if off quick? Maybe a flap hanging down over it?"

"I've got the new IIFS, which includes the tactical load-bearing vest, alpine pack and a little patrol pack. Everything goes in it or attaches to it, including your sleeping bag and sidearm. You can move and fight in it, if you need to. I can rig the other weapons to that. These new materials are magic. They even make human ligaments out of Gore-tex now."

I remembered my own knee and made a mental note to stop at a drugstore for a couple of Ace knee bandages.

"You want the flak vests, Grenada model?"

I shook my head. It was too hot. Dykstra seemed to approve.

"Now you realize," he continued, "that some of these hog and deer hunters carry military weapons. I could put you behind a nice M-21 with image intensifier. Those H and K people make several nice sniper rifles. You could even pack an M-16 and go full auto out there, and people wouldn't know it wasn't one of those AR-15 civilian clones unless you fired it that way."

"I'd just rather not look military," I said. "I got a feeling the only people back in there are people we don't want to see us. If they do see us, we want to look like a couple of city putzes with more equipment than brains."

"You're on the right track," Dykstra said, allowing himself a chuckle to match his cheeks. "Most hunters don't backpack these days. They have their four-wheelers and they're home for supper. 'Course you're going into wilderness where they don't allow vehicles."

"And so we look dopey and they decide it's better to let us go by and die out there," I said. "Now, we need to see in the dark."

"Everything's possible in the modern world of weapons," he said. "I've got some PVS-5 goggles here in the shop. Entirely legal. I've got a pair of Steiner binoculars you can use to find your target. They weigh about three pounds, but they're incredible with just a little available light. Good for daytime, too, and they'll give you range and bearing. I assume there's going to be some available light where you're going."

I thought about the mine. "There's one place we may have to work without even starlight."

"You switch the goggles to infrared projection for that. They may see some tiny red dots where your eyes are, but that's all. May I assume this is a somewhat closed space?"

"Yes. But some of it's open country."

"I recommend a laser light sight on the Uzi."

"We don't want to kill anybody." It was Happy's voice.

"My, my," Dykstra said in a carefully condescending tone. "You're certainly shopping for some dangerous hardware."

"The idea is to have it if we need it," I said. "There are innocent people with them."

"All the more reason for accurate sighting. And the

deer rifle might give you the option of picking somebody off without killing them. It's a small caliber and if you can hit a leg . . . ."

"You got stun guns?" I asked.

"Yeah, but if you're dealing with a lot of people you're not going to buy yourself much time. They start pulling out of the paralysis in a few minutes. By the way, there's a time problem with those combat goggles. Anywhere over thirty minutes, you run the risk of your eyes just shutting down. They're a terrible strain, so you gotta wrap it up pretty quick. I recommend gas."

"Ai, chihuahua," Leila said.

Dykstra gave her an appropriate grimace. "Nonlethal, of course," he said. "I think I can lay my hands on some B-2, and I know I've got two good, cheap Israeli masks adaptable to the goggles. You lay that stuff in there right and everybody's tripping by the time you show. You can do it with a fogger, which is a little heavier to pack but really lays it down, or with grenades. It has an effect a lot like LSD. Tear gas is almost as debilitating and very easy to get. Either way, the whole bunch is out of the play and you can walk through and figure out who's been naughty and who's been nice."

"They have dogs."

"The Uzi," he said. He seemed to be wondering silently if we were squeamish about killing animals. "Or pack in some cyanide burgers. Or drug some meat if you don't want to kill the dogs."

"We're getting overloaded here as it is," I said.

"Now there's the chemical option," Dykstra said. "GZS. Find their water supply and everybody passes out, wakes up, throws up, goes where you tell them."

"They won't all drink at the same time."

"Good psy-war op. The others worry what's happening. They always think disease, never strategy."

"Jesus Christ," Leila said. "Chemical warfare! This stinks!"

"It's kinder than bullets," Dykstra said. "Nobody dies. That's with the nonlethal stuff. There's also the lethal nonpersistent—kills but then loses its strength."

"Can you get me some of the nonlethal?" I asked.

"Take four, five days. Somewhat controversial stuff. But it worked in 'Nam."

Leila hissed.

"We don't have that long," I said.

"Too bad," he said.

"I want a cover for when we go in. I want them to think fire."

"I've got smoke grenades in assorted colors. The prettier ones were used in 'Nam to mark LZs."

"White or gray or black," I said.

"I've only got white."

"Fine. And if we get the right wind we lay the smoke and giggle gas down at the same time. Can you get me some stun grenades? We may have a lot of resistance from a mine shaft where we won't have time to wait for the gas. The grenades could solve that problem."

He thought about it. "Flashbangers are hard to get, but I've got a couple left. Personal hardware. We played with them a while back. I'll let you have 'em, but you realize that your friendlies may suffer some temporary damage to eardrums or eyesight if you use these. There are some real hazards. And either these or the smokers are a big fire risk out there now."

"I'd like to use the smokers on the river bank, if I get the right wind. The others inside a mine shaft."

"Sounds containable."

"Sounds like the G. Gordon Fucking Liddy Camp for Outdoor Crazies, is what it sounds like!" Leila said.

Dykstra gave her a cherubic smile with the lower half of his face and a Die Bitch look with his eyes. Happy shook his head in dismay. "I think this op is taking shape," I said, feeling more than a little silly. "How much?"

He whipped out his calculator. "Uzi, laser sights," he muttered, like some Victorian clerk counting out beans and sealing wax. "That's maybe the least legal piece of hardware involved here, by the way—a class-three weapon. You didn't get it here. Rifle, shotgun, suppressors for Uzi and rifle, IIFS times two, smoke grenades, stun grenades, gas—these would also be much frowned on by the feds—starlight scope—and you're getting a deal on that—Steiner binocs, two pairs goggles, gas masks. . . . Do you have your own backpacks and other gear?"

"No. And my friend will need a good knife—a K-Bar will do."

"K-Bar knife—like everything else, in the matte finish—two backpacks, sleeping bags, canteens. . . . I'll outfit the whole op, including ammo, web gear, MREs, trail mix and toilet paper for—"

He named a figure that shouldn't have surprised me but did anyway.

"What's an MRE?" Leila asked. "Some other deadly shit?"

"Meal Ready to Eat," Dykstra said. "I like 'em better than C-rations or the LRRP freeze-dried stuff. You even get little fruit cups. All the pleasures of home, without the hassles."

Leila knew what or whom he meant by hassles. She snorted.

"That's quite a figure," I said.

"Minus ten percent discount because you're a fellow professional and another five because you're recommended by a friend." He named the new figure. Sarah Diehl would soon qualify as a war lord, but it was a lot less than even my backcountry geeks would ask for ransom in these inflationary times. He gave me the wire address and then told me where to meet him that night, at a shopping center on the west side of Redding. "I'll have it packed for you and covered in paper or cardboard. You can check and repack if you like. You'll need to get a feel for where everything is. It's just my suggestion about where everything will pack best. So all you have to do is transfer it to your car, stop somewhere later and get acquainted with it in good light, and you're ready."

We shook hands. I went to the phone and called Sarah at her friend's. She said she wasn't sure she could get a wire off that day. It was after five and Western Union might be closed. She didn't even question the amount. I had her hold and went to explain that to Dykstra, who was putting the laser sight on an Uzi.

"Look," he said. "I don't have to be mysterious with you guys. You're highly recommended. I know the money will come. I know time's important to you, so let's put the stuff together here. I'll run you through each piece and we'll pack it and you'll be ready to go first light tomorrow."

He surprised me. I thanked him. Even Leila seemed softened by his hardware generosity.

He waved off our gratitude. "I'm covered. This Uzi doesn't happen to be registered. I bought it from one of those Kudzu survival cats the last time I was in Atlanta. A great gun town. He was hurting for lawyer money. The gas and other goodies aren't registered, either. Your timing is good. So your sponsor goes to the Union first thing East Coast time and the money's there when my office opens. Otherwise, I figure you stiffed me. I have your tag number, your service connection, your private cop license. I get everybody's driver's license number right now tonight, and when the money don't come I report a theft of certain weapons which are perfectly legal for me to own, but not for you to steal or use. I say I saw you driving away in a northwesterly direction. They catch you somewhere. But it won't come to that."

We were all somewhat less impressed with his generosity then, but we gave him our driver's licenses and I gave him my PI ticket. While he recorded them I called Sarah back and explained the importance of getting the wire off early, and told her to call Dykstra if there was any problem. He returned our licenses and issued hunting licenses to Happy and me. Then we took everything to the firing range and practiced with our tools.

Dykstra showed Happy how to use the K-Bar. Like me, Happy was unhappy with knives. Dykstra showed him how to take a sentry from behind so that he can't cry out. There are several schools of thought on that, including, I suppose, the throat cutting you see in movies, but whether you take the trachea with the jugular through the jugular notch, the brain from behind, just above the highest cervical vertebra, the heart or kidney from behind, or other options, you must, Dykstra explained as Leila grew paler, be sure to disable either the nervous system or the breathing of the victim—trachea, lungs—so that he either cannot signal his body to scream or lacks the wind to do it. "You're not movie slashers," he told us. "Don't waste blade." Only Dykstra enjoyed that demonstration.

I brought in my government Colt and the Brazilian 9 mm for Happy. I insisted that Leila fire a few rounds with the .357 and then keep it in her purse. We got more ammunition for the pistols. We worked with them for a while, then the rifle, the shotgun, and the Uzi.

We got a little giddy, as even the least warlike men can when firing weapons. We went outside to try the binoculars, the scope, the night goggles. We walked up to Leila wearing the goggles, pretending to be aliens. We asked her if she'd seen Norris or Stallone. We thought it might relieve the tension. She sat in the front seat with her arms folded, staring straight ahead, pretending we weren't there.

Twenty-two

Leila dropped us at the lumber company fence about eight that morning. It wasn't very professional, maybe, but it was the earliest we could make it. I'd bought a couple of knee wraps the night before, and a flashlight. We had the forest service map and a machete from Happy's garage. All we needed was more equipment. We got the backpacks into place and looked at each other in dismay. Happy pretended that his legs were slowly collapsing. He was getting back some of his sense of humor. Strange time for that. We moved around outside the fence. I practiced taking the Uzi from behind his pack and returning it. Dykstra had rigged slings and hooks on the pack frames for the rifle and shotgun, but they were still part of the weight.

I took mine off and went over to the Eagle. I tried to kiss Leila through the window, then pulled her out and kissed her truly and well, putting my back against the warm hood and pulling her against me. "I'm so scared," she said. "I couldn't stand for anything to happen to you."

"We've got enough equipment to take on an army," I said.

"Sure," she said, "but can you carry it?"

"We'll hire Sherpas," I said. "And Gurkhas."

She started to crack wise, then just lowered her head, then raised it and hugged me with a fierceness and strength that pleased me. Then she tried to push me away and get into the car. Her face was flushed and her eyes were getting wet.

"Listen," I said. "Come here on the second morning from now. Maybe you shouldn't bring Martha and Becky until we know what we got." I looked back at Happy and he nodded, no longer playful. "If we're not here by then, give us one more day, and if we're not here that morning, call the sheriff, state police, everybody. Carry that pistol with you at all times. Keep your doors locked once you get near Gancy. By morning I mean between eight and noon. Don't come before and don't stay after. If we should get out before with them, they may still have the keys to this rental—if somebody hasn't siphoned all the gas." I went over and pushed against the rear of the little Dodge and heard it slosh. The geeks were probably using it for a gas depot. "If we have to run, we can break a window and hotwire this, can't we, Ace?" Happy nodded, still not smiling.

"I think I'll stay with Becky and Martha," she said. "You could reach me there."

"And Sarah can reach you. Listen."

"What?"

"All I want you to do is sit here between eight and noon with the doors locked. Anybody bothers you, shoot him and drive away."

She nodded. I reached in and kissed her again and she started the car. Happy went over the fence and I handed him the packs. We started along the trail.

Like pack mules. No, worse. We had no tails to switch the flies. Mules probably carried less weight. Within a mile, I was already thinking about what we could do without. Real commandos traveled light. But real commandos didn't know they only had something less than twenty safe miles and a few more hard ones to travel before they set up a camp. Then we might need any of our gear, and since we hadn't seen the place, we didn't know which.

Happy and I talked a little at first. Mainly it was just the kind of quick question from the past that occurs to friends walking to a war of some kind.

"Honest to God," he said. "You ever make it with Beth?"

"No. Yes. No—"

"You're doing it again! After all these years."

"The answer is an unequivocal maybe."

"Damn your ass."

"Vanity, vanity. And profanity. You make it with Sarah? You're the reformed guy here, so I know you'll tell the truth."

"No, I didn't, as God as my witness," Happy said smugly.

"Good. I was banging Beth all the time. I thought I was gonna break the couch with her."

"Bastard," he said. He was laughing, though.

"No, truth is I never did."

"I'll never be able to believe you now."

"Believe me up here," I said, looking down the road. "That's the only way it's going to work."

We crossed the river and followed the trail, hoping to see any fellow travelers in time to get off it and let them pass without seeing us. The land was usually not too steep nearest the river, and there was often enough cover from the stunted pines and black oaks to do that. Happy showed me the Madroña tree—a very hard wood called Madrone by most Anglos, with slick, peeled-looking red bark—the manzanita, wild azalea, and buck brush. California jays sounded their alarms at us, and those same, open-beaked, ominous crows marked our way like warnings. When I mentioned them Happy said they were ravens, larger wilderness birds with a rougher feathering at the throat and a different shape to the tail.

It looked to me like a choice between traveling the river bed and being seen or bushwhacking across the ridges, hoping to be able to look down when we were above the tree line and get our bearings. The slopes between river and ridge were too steep to travel. We stopped every mile or so, but we didn't touch the water until noon, when we ate some trail mix, swatted some flies and sipped very carefully from one of our jugs. I was still wearing the Rolex I'd been issued in the Navy. Finally, I had a real mission. Happy cut a length of Madrone with his new knife for a walking stick. Then he cut me one. It was hard going, that wood, and I wanted to tell him to save his energy.

But they came in handy. When we got to the pass between Flattop and Bread Loaf Mountains, we found a place to ford the river and began the climb to the far ridge, where I thought we might be able to travel unseen. But I heard a shout and we stopped and crouched. We were concealed. Maybe they were shouting at something else. I heard a dog bark. Happy turned to give me the Uzi and I turned for him to reach the binoculars from the top of my pack. He crawled down just past the manzanita which hid us and found a view of the river. He watched while I crawled down to the other side of the bush, then handed me the binoculars. I laid the Uzi on a patch of dry pine needles and had a look.

There were two dogs ranging along the far river bank, obviously on our scent. Two men watched them, their eyes moving everywhere. Both were carrying shotguns. They looked a little like Indians, very desperate Indians. They were wearing loincloths and headbands. One dog was large boned and tan. The other looked like one of those coyote half-breeds you see out here. The dogs didn't cross the river and the men moved back into the trees. We were in the Land of the People Who Live Like the Hoopa.

The climb to the ridge was grueling. We lost our footing often and fell sliding on pine needles with all our gear until we hit a friendly tree. It was so steep that we often had to pull ourselves along from one tree trunk to the next. We weren't aware of sweating in the dry heat, but I knew we were. The dry air sucked up the moisture as it came, and salt caked on our skin. We were both very thirsty, but there was no room to maneuver and open the packs. We just kept climbing. I led with the machete, but there wasn't that much to clear, so I stowed it and just pulled myself from tree to tree, looking always at my feet for the next bare earth or outcrop of rock for a foothold. Happy followed, still using his Madrone stick.

I heard him grunt and turned to watch him slide on his belly until he held out the stick and caught two tree trunks at either end of it to hold him. Then he chinned his way forward until he could get a footing and came ahead. I hadn't thought to ask him if he had good boots; he was wearing black high-top sneakers. Right out of our childhood. Most of our childhood was back in fashion. Punk was back. But I didn't think it was what we needed out here. I wondered what the rattlers were doing at this elevation during this strange, unseasonal weather.

It was mid-afternoon by the time we reached the ridge. This one was not so high as others farther along. The map and the trees we found there suggested that we could travel it upriver in concealment for some distance, then gain the next ridge without doing too much more climbing. All we had to do was keep the river on our right. Of course we couldn't see it and couldn't hear it, but it had to be down that slippery slope we'd just climbed. We walked along in silence most of the way. We were on a water break when Happy said: "I'm not afraid."

"I'm not either," I said. I was thinking that it must have been a lot worse to be a conventional soldier and leave your warm tent before dawn to face enemy rifles and cannon. To charge across a field at the enemy or face his charge: That's one kind of fighting. The electronic and nuclear warrior seldom sees his enemy; the enemy is just a target in the sight of a guidance system, and so is he. He never knows the reality unless his plane or ship or position is hit, and then it's over too fast to be afraid. Like the video game that tells you you're already dead. That's another kind of fighting. This was a third kind.

"Why aren't we scared?" he asked.

"One reason is that we haven't really had time to think about fighting. We've been planning and packing and busting ass to get here. Another is that this kind of warfare is such a nasty, physical bitch that by the time you find the enemy you're grateful. Fighting is a relief. You don't have to sit on your ass in the boonies and feed bugs for a while."

We stowed the water bottles and moved on until our ridge ended. The gap between the ridges was greater than I'd expected. It was a wash for the spring runoff from the higher mountains beyond. It was dry now and much higher than the river it fed in spring, but it was hard going, too. We wound our way through rocks and rough gravel, our ankles twisting at each step. My knee hurt. Happy had to be feeling those rocks through his sneakers, but he didn't complain.

We came up out of it along a more friendly rise which was gradual and had decent footing and led to a higher ridge above the tree line where we could make better time. We could now see Devil's Horns Mountain at an angle to us. The Midnight Mine and their camp were where the mountain met the river. We were above it now, and we looked for a view of the river. Our luck had been getting better all afternoon. Sometimes it's like that after you make a full commitment to something. That's why Cortez burned his ships, giving his men the choice of conquering New Spain or being eaten by the Aztecs. We found an outcropping of rock just above where we thought they should be. It raised us above the treetops below and gave us a look at the far bank. When there was any wind and when it came our way, we could smell the urine odor of a meth lab. Maybe it would confuse their dogs.

There had been a fire down our side—probably from lightning and drowned by rain before it got too far. It had cleared the trees along the slope leading up to our vantage point, and the newer growth wasn't so high. More luck. We ate our MREs and watched. We took turns with the binoculars. Tonight's menu was chicken à la king, broccoli and cheese, the promised fruit cup and a big piece of cake—all of it plastic wrapped, light weight, and very welcome. A guaranteed 3,800 calories.

Before sunset a woman came down to fill a water can. Then she pulled off her cotton dress and waded out to wash herself with surprising dignity and delicacy in the slow and shallow river. She seemed to have a small cake of soap which she handled like a treasure. She had light brown hair, a flat face, and enormous breasts. She milked herself. There was an infant back there who didn't drink enough of her milk. There were tattooed chains at her wrists and ankles, and fruit tattooed on her heavy buttocks—something red on the left and something yellow on the right. She toweled herself and stood for a time letting her hair dry, enjoying the coolness.

We heard raucous laughter and dogs barking. Two men came down from the trees. I could see smoke now from above and found a lightning-killed pine to mark it. The men looked like extras from the cast of *Road Warrior* who'd been abandoned in the Australian outback. Both were carrying M-16s, which they leaned against a boulder. One wore a sombrero, a dungaree vest, and studded leather wrist bands. The other had a red bandanna headband and tattoos on his face cheeks. The dominant dog was a heavy, black rottweiler and the second was a reddish hound. The woman tried to put her dress back on, but one of the men grabbed her.

She accepted his touch. She closed her eyes while he bent and suckled her breasts. The other man was taking a crap on the river bank. When he finished, he pulled up his jeans without any effort to clean himself and used a stick to propel his feces into the river. He stepped out onto a rock and used his right hand to make waves toward it, washing it more quickly downstream toward the Hoopa and civilization. He laughed. The other man stopped suckling to see what he'd done and laughed with him. They gave the finger to everything downriver.

Then they made the woman kneel on her towel and fucked her. The suckler mounted her first. The second man came up from the river and put himself into her mouth. She moved her hair back from over her forehead and sucked him. The other man finished and the one from the river moved around to mount her. The towel wasn't long enough and her huge breasts sagged and swayed and rubbed against the rocks. She cupped them in her hands to protect them, propped on her elbows. The second man ejaculated onto her back while the first one laughed. She shielded both breasts with one arm and lowered her head onto the other to rest while they pulled up their jeans, snatched their rifles, and went back to camp.

After a while she stood up. Her face was entirely blank. She stood like someone who had forgotten her destination. Then she found her little soap, waded out and washed again briefly as the sun began its descent behind us, pulled her dress over her head and hurried back to camp.

I'd given Happy the binoculars once, but he'd handed them right back. I was trying to get a better view of camp before dark when I saw some movement to the right and then a skinny man in mechanic's coveralls climbing one of the bigger pine trees with an M-16 to what I realized was a concealed platform, a blind, an observation post. I tried to figure their strategy. I doubted that they expected him to see trouble at night. What was he doing up there? A very fat guy with a red beard came down to set a couple of primitive traps along the trail. He wore overalls. The trap nearest the river was just rocks in cans on a wire across the trail, higher than the dogs. The one nearest the camp was a spring-loaded Malayan rake trap with a trip wire and sharpened Madrone stakes. I marked its location. It looked as though it might work, but I wasn't much impressed by the security here.

Maybe there was more, but Devil's Horns Mountain protected their rear, so their trouble had to come either across the river, along the river trail, or through that densely wooded open side of the triangle whose other sides were made by the mountain and the river. This was the land between them and the Hoopas. They'd apparently convinced the Hoopas to leave them alone, and the only easy way to get this far was through the Hoopas. If we tried to come in that way, we'd have to worry about the Hoopas, too. Maybe they had mines back in there, but the dogs might set them off and I figured the dogs were the best security they had, if the meth fumes hadn't burned out their noses. Probably just more of those spring traps, covered holes with punji sticks, and primitive stuff like that. They used the river so much, they couldn't put them there, which explained the guy in the tree. Maybe he was supposed to stay awake or stand watches with other people, but what he likely did was sleep up there all night and, if the dogs sounded, started firing the M-16 and rousing the others. If they had enough weapons back in that mine, they could hold out pretty well.

"How could animals like that have children?" Happy worried.

"*Because* they're animals," I said. "We ought to require licenses, like with guns. Margaret Mead recommended that, and she knows her primitives."

"It's too easy to get guns," Happy said.

"And children," I said. "If children were harder to get, maybe we wouldn't be so free with guns."

The sun set brilliantly and quickly. Happy missed it. He was facing the river, worrying. When it was dark enough I fumbled and found the Steiners and swept the bank. They were good, worth hauling even at three pounds. I tried the rifle night scope. It was good enough to pick him off, but not as clear and detailed as the Steiners. Everything had a green and ghostly tint through the scope. I studied the sentry in his blind, the crosshairs suggesting a strange and powerful point of view. I saw his cigarette smoke and that of a campfire back in the woods, where the mine was. We had a waxing quarter moon. Just about the right light for us and not enough for them. I thought of Jennifer. I'd never met Chris.

"Could we go tonight?" Happy asked.

"We'd better wait. We don't know enough. We haven't seen the kids. And we don't know how many freaks there are."

"I feel so helpless."

"Sometimes waiting kills your enemy." I think I'd read that in a samurai book.

"I'm going to pray," he said. "If you think it's silly, you're wrong."

"Maybe I'll pray, too," I said, but I didn't.

Twenty-three

It was a miserable night. The bugs killed us a few cells at a time. I don't know where mosquitos come from in country and weather like that, but they came. The one thing we'd forgotten was bug repellant. We put camouflage makeup on our hands and faces instead. Dykstra had included it to help us hide from our human enemies, but maybe it would fool bugs. It didn't help much. I knew how Happy felt. I began to think about running down with the Uzi blazing. I stood watch for a while. I didn't see the sentry smoke again, so I judged he was asleep. Around eleven I let myself try to doze. There was nothing else to do and we would need the rest.

It was a miserable day. But I think we got a decent count of who was down there: There were two more guys we hadn't seen—a small black guy who seemed seriously confused but was carrying a shotgun and so figured as one of them, and a tall, freckled fellow with a bleached yellow Mohawk growing out. He looked like a psychedelic broom. That meant six guys: the shitter and the suckler at the river, the skinny sentry in mechanic's overalls, the fat guy—whom I'd come to call Haystack—the spacy black, and the broom. We'd already seen the wet nurse. We saw three other women come to the river that day. One was a frail-looking pregnant blonde, another a black-haired Indian girl and the third a rat-faced girl with a shaved head who we thought was a guy until she took off her shorts and T-shirt and waded in to cool off. She was just barely female at that. And baby made eleven.

I wondered how eleven such campers could intimidate the entire pseudo-Hoopa Nation. Maybe there were only two Hoopas, with shotguns. Maybe some of this group was out of town, or rather *in* town to get supplies or use the phone. Maybe there were some who hadn't come down to the river, though in this heat I doubted it. Or maybe they were just so nasty that the quasi-Hoopas prefered an uneasy peace to a big fight for all this desolate wilderness.

About eleven the spacy black guy brought Jennifer and Chris down to the river with large, steel water cans. Happy stiffened like a bird dog with scent. The kids looked dirty but unharmed. Jennifer waited while Chris filled the cans. The black guy came up to her in a strangely mechanical way and reached under her T-shirt, his shotgun held by its barrel in his right hand. Chris came up the bank and yanked his hand away and put him into a wristlock. It was a bad move but it worked. The black guy forgot he was carrying a weapon and when Chris let off the pressure, he turned and began walking away from the river, as though he'd forgotten his duty.

The kids looked across the river in our direction, obviously wondering if they could make it. I began to wonder if this could be the time. It would take us several minutes to get down to the river, longer for them to climb up to us while we covered them. Then we'd have armed people chasing us through a wilderness they knew better than we did. Suddenly the black guy turned and ran toward them. He ran right up to Chris and put the barrel of the shotgun against his nose. Chris stood still. I could hear Happy's breath. Then the black guy lowered the gun and the kids finished their task and followed him up the path with the cans.

"Let's go now," Happy said in a snaky voice.

"Strategy," I reminded him. "It's the wrong time, and we don't know enough."

"We know they're there, and in danger."

"They're fine," I said.

We heard the sound of an engine from downriver. The noise grew louder. Down the dry part of the river bed came an old Harley with a sidecar. It was a rocky ride. The hog pilot had a long, bandito moustache. The guy in the sidecar had long, blond hair like a Viking, a couple of big, plastic supermarket bags bouncing in his lap, and an M-16. At their approach, everybody came down to the river, including the spacy black guy and our two kids. The bikers stopped at the beginning of the path and turned off the hog.

The Bandito got off and walked over to have some words with Jennifer. She shrugged. He raised his hand in a threatening gesture. We could hear pieces of words, like scraps of paper blown across by the wind. You could see the tension in Chris's body. The Bandito turned to look at him; he was not happy. Chris met his gaze. Jennifer did some more talking. She was working hard at it. We couldn't hear it, but we could watch it take effect. She was telling the Bandito what he wanted to hear.

Meanwhile, the Viking was passing out a few goodies he'd bought at the Safeway, like a suburban dad home from a week on the road. Most of the excitement was about three bottles of Jack Daniel's.

"Lucky for us these people don't have much of an attention span," I whispered.

"They must have tried to call Sarah," Happy whispered back.

"Our timing is good," I said. We pulled back to the far

side of our rock where we could talk. "I think we've seen them all," I said. "We've got eight men and four women. There's the Bandito, the Viking, the spacy black Brother, the Shitter, the Suckler, the Mechanic sentry, the Broom, and Haystack. Four women: the Wet Nurse, the pregnant Blonde, the Indian, and Rat Face."

"And the baby," Happy said.

"Right. If there is a baby. Maybe it died and they're using her for milk. These people are a little different. But we'll try to be careful."

"We'll have to be careful. If we shoot in the mine—"

"I don't want to shoot in the mine. We could kill the kids. Now that we know who everybody is, here's how I think we do it."

I laid it out for him. He made some suggestions. We modified and refined it. We finally agreed. Then we took turns standing watch, the free man limbering up behind the ridge or napping in the partial shade of our rock. We were sore. The rocks were making themselves comfortable in our bodies. But in about twelve hours, we'd be ready to do the thing we came here to do.

There wasn't much activity that afternoon. The heat sent everybody looking for shade. The guys had moved the Harley up the path into the camp. Before sunset Rat Face came down for water—for the bourbon, maybe. Everybody else was hidden to us. We ate our MREs and drank some water. Tonight was Beef Stroganoff.

We heard an occasional voice because the wind was in our direction. For now it was great; it kept our scent from the dogs; later I needed to have it blow their way. Happy didn't like the fact that their voices were higher, louder, from drinking. He worried what that would mean for the kids. They played a portable tape player—late Doobie Brothers—until the batteries ran down. This group was an eloquent argument for sterilizing Michael McDonald fans. We heard him doing his four-note range, blue-eyed soul riffs at slower and slower speeds. We heard somebody smash the tape player. We heard cursing and more laughter.

"You've heard of hard rock mining," I whispered. "These people are hard-core soft pop." Happy wasn't in a joking mood. I agreed there wasn't much to cheer us now. The kids were alive, but beyond our reach. And it seemed very unlikely that Jennifer was still unmolested. They had a motive for keeping her alive, but none for respecting her. I kept that to myself.

The Shitter came staggering down about eight and climbed into the sentry box. He held a flashlight as he climbed, and its beam ranged crazily through the trees and across the river to us until he finally gained his perch and turned it off. They were smart enough not to use their flashlight batteries on the tape player. Haystack had followed him with his own flashlight. He set the traps and made his elephantine way back up the path, too large to stagger.

I suggested to Happy that we rest as much as we could. Neither of us felt like talking. Around midnight the wind shifted toward them and I began to feel lucky. The dogs barked a little, then stopped. I was so pleased with that, I fell asleep. I was surprised to wake about three, surprised that I could have been relaxed enough to sleep at all. Happy was awake and I knew he hadn't slept. It was his son down there. I remembered Scott Fitzgerald's Dark Night of the Soul, when it's always three in the morning. This was close enough. The wind still favored us. We put on our gas masks and goggles and went behind the ridge to limber up some more. Now everything looked greenish and hi-tech ghostly, like through the night scope. We tried the infrared light projectors in a dark place near the big rock. It looked the same, only the infrared boosted the image. I saw red pinpoints where Happy's eyes were.

We rested our eyes. Then it was time. Almost four. The lowest ebb of human consciousness. I checked with the Steiners for any signs. Nothing from the sentry tree. Since they hadn't reached Sarah, they had no reason to think anyone knew what they'd done. The harvest was sold. They had some whiskey. They wouldn't be expecting us.

We made our way slowly down to the river and waded across. I was mid-river when it hit me what an impossible situation this was. I stopped for a second and Happy's gas mask turned toward me. I was afraid—not so much of being physically hurt but of being a fool. That's always been the big risk for me. A fool with a king's ransom's worth of hi-tech hardware and a shiver down his spine now to match this cold river. I knew I had to start moving again. I couldn't let Happy know how badly I wished to be home. I was grateful for the mask and grateful for the smoke grenade I fumbled for and found in my jacket. I remembered the Claymore mines we'd used in training, which had printed on their business end the practical Armed Forces advice: THIS SIDE TOWARD ENEMY. Soldiers had to keep it simple, I remembered. Happy waved me on and I found that I could follow.

We heard the first dog just as we were setting the smoke and gas grenades. We were lucky they hadn't come at us sooner, with the wind blowing toward them since midnight. Maybe we'd been there so long that they'd adjusted to us as one of the camp smells.

The rottweiler came very fast and gave me no options. I put the laser dot on him and ripped him with Uzi, and the other dogs dug in, turned, and ran. His brief yelp was louder than the suppressed weapon. I hadn't wanted to do that. He might have been the best creature in that camp. I covered the sentry tree while Happy disarmed the traps with his Madrone stick and knife. The Shitter might be too high for the gas to reach in time. I was getting nervous about him.

Maybe he smelled the smoke, although it hadn't reached him yet. Maybe he heard the dog or the Uzi. Maybe he was just getting up to piss. But up he got, so I dealt with him. This way I could see him and know what I was not shooting at. I fired all around his blind, trying not to hit him. He didn't know what was happening except that there was this red-orange laser beam flitting about like Tinker Bell and his tree hut was exploding almost silently all around him.

He jumped. He was about thirty feet above the very hard ground, so he knocked himself out. I ran over and dragged him into the path of the gas. I pulled the magazine from his M-16, ejected the shell he had chambered, and threw the magazine and rifle in different directions. I could see a bone sticking out behind his upper arm.

I joined Happy on the trail, threw more of the gas grenades toward the camp, and we came in fast with the smoke. It seemed at first that nobody was awake. Then we heard somebody yell "Fire!"

We were right among them. They seemed to have been sleeping in the open around the dead campfire. They couldn't see us. Nobody had found his flashlight yet, and we just walked among them, watching them smile and sit back down. Some had never gotten up—they just smiled and rolled over. I found the Wet Nurse, holding her baby. I ushered her out beyond the heaviest gas and helped her lie down with the baby in the crook of her arm. As in the stories you hear about Indian babies, it never cried, even before the gas. I don't know who she thought I was. I went back to the others. They smelled bad, but they felt good. The plan seemed to be working, but we hadn't counted everybody yet. It was eerie being able to see in their darkness, walking among them like invisible aliens.

The pregnant Blonde was having a bad trip. Dykstra hadn't mentioned this possibility. She'd found her flashlight and then found me with it. I moved toward her quickly, the light in my face until I could get close enough to knock it aside. She was screaming for help. I wanted to help her out of the gas. She was also holding a big knife above her head and brought it down with all the desperation in her skinny arm toward me. I didn't want to risk her baby, but I had to keep from being stabbed.

I stepped back and she missed, screaming all the time. I dropped the Uzi. She ran at me with the knife, and I caught it with both hands, twisted it to my right, and stepped under it to bar her arm over my shoulder. I hesitated, while she scratched and pulled at me with amazing strength. I was afraid of hurting her, but she'd already tied me up longer than anybody else. All this high tech and I'm undone by a skinny pregnant woman. Happy came up and hit her in the jaw with his fist, and she folded like a bad kite. I dragged her out to join the nursing mother and child.

I ran back to recover the Uzi, but before I could pick it up Happy yelled and tossed me his stick. It didn't make sense. He'd left his shotgun somewhere and was now empty-handed, and we'd forgotten to gas the mine. We were really screwing up. I threw a gas grenade into the mine shaft and almost immediately the Viking and Bandito came stumbling out cursing and waving their M-16s. Happy stepped inside the Bandito's rifle and punched him to the throat, then snatched the weapon away. The Viking was on my side, looking in the darkness and smoke for a target. I knocked his rifle barrel down with the stick and hit him in the face—a solid triple, at least—before he could raise it again or even fire a round. Happy had thrown the Bandito's weapon aside and was working on him with his fists. He was fierce, like the old days, like Christ among the moneychangers. Then, just as he'd finished the duking of Bandito, Haystack came roaring up from the mine like a bear and grabbed Happy from behind.

I picked up the Uzi but kept the stick, too, watching the mine while Happy dealt with Haystack. I hoped his mask was intact. I hoped nobody else would come from the mine. I hoped Haystack would be folding anytime from the gas, but he didn't seem to be breathing much. Of course, neither was Happy in that grip. Everything was this otherworldly green, and things seemed to move in slow motion. My struggling friend looked like some red-eyed alien rat in the grip of a professional wrestler. This was not what I'd planned.

Happy tried to butt backwards with his head, but Haystack's head was beyond reach, and Happy risked knocking his mask loose that way. I pushed the Uzi over my shoulder to hang by its sling behind me and laid the stick across Haystack's kidneys, then, as he released Happy and sank to his knees, across the base of his skull. He fell forward, his face in the dirt. I went to him and turned it to the side, so he could breathe, and saw that the gas had finally reached him and he was smiling.

We ran toward the mouth of the mine. We'd figured that they wouldn't be very far inside it. We didn't have an accurate count, but everybody out here was quiet. Then we heard a shotgun fired inside. No choice. I threw in a stun grenade and we turned the infrared switches and followed it. The mine was full of gunsmoke and the terrible, metallic smell of fresh blood. The black Brother was in there, his back against solid rock, his face and most of his head gone. Blood still pumped from his neck. The shotgun was propped in his lap. Maybe he'd been working up to that most of his life.

The kids were sitting just beyond, looking at us in the way of people who have had a very hard time and have come to accept their fates. Then I realized they were unconscious. They were bleeding from the nose and probably from the ears. I could see a rough-carpentered table beyond where the Midnight Miners were trying to learn how to manufacture amphetamines. I'd heard it was pretty simple chemistry but I still didn't think they were smart enough, and if they delivered a bad batch to the Hell's Angels this cave wasn't deep enough to hide them.

Happy fussed over the kids while I secured the people outside, using rope I found in the cave and tying them the way I'd been taught, elbows together behind the back, then the wrists. I tied the wet nurse's feet instead. Later I'd rope them all together by the neck. The gas was dissipating pretty quickly, but the meth pee smell would last a long time down there.

When I got back inside the mine, the kids were coming to. Happy had just been watching them helplessly. They couldn't see us. They were both crying in a strangely dispassionate way. They'd just been through the shotgun, then the flashbanger. If they could have seen us they would have seen two strangers with rat-eye goggles and rat-face masks. They were holding each other. Happy touched Chris and the boy shrank away.

"Tell him who you are," I said. The masks muffled our voices.

"It's your dad," Happy said. "Chris, it's me."

Chris recognized the voice, even through the mask. He got up and groped his way toward his father until they could grab each other. Jennifer stayed seated against the wall, her hands probing delicately outward for more information. I reached down and took her hands. "Quite an adventure," I said.

"Who are you?" she asked.

"Your mother's hip friend," I said.

Twenty-Four

We made quite a parade at the river the next morning. We let Chris ride the Harley, with Jennifer and our extra weapons in the sidecar. Happy and I would guard the string of Midnight Miners whom we'd tied and hobbled and strung together with their own rope. Happy would walk point and I'd come behind the column. The Shitter was in a lot of pain with his fractured arm and Viking whimpered about the nose and face bones I'd broken, but everybody was healthy enough to walk out, including the pregnant Amazon, now calmer, and the Wet Nurse with her baby. We made the healthiest guys carry the rest of our gear. We'd found Jennifer's credit cards in the cave, along with the rental car keys, some small change, and her Cartier watch with the mauve suede band. The three surviving dogs brought up the rear as we got ready to walk out through the Land of Those Who Live Like the Hoopa.

But first, Rat Face, who was near me at the end of the column, began hissing and motioning me over. Her gestures were wild and intimate until I got near her; then she turned her head and spoke to the space beside me: "That fucker Lane did it," she said furiously. "He made Mose do it. That's why Mose killed himself. He was supposed to kill the kids too if anything happened."

"What did Lane make Mose do?" I asked. Mose had to be the black guy.

"Untie me for a while. I'll show you."

"Who's Lane?"

She pointed ahead to the Bandito, who was pale now and might have sweated visibly if it weren't so dry. He tried to approach us and tripped Haystack, who stumbled, cursed, growled, and jerked on Lane's ropes, tripping him to the ground.

"Happy, hold the gun on these people," I said. "This woman wants to show me something."

I untied Rat Face and followed her to a piece of clear ground behind the camp. She found a spade against a nearby oak and started digging in the soft earth. Chris came up and took it from her and dug while she and I watched. Jennifer stayed down in the sidecar. It was a shallow grave. I was surprised that the animals hadn't disturbed it. We smelled him before we saw him. When the face was clear, Chris said "Oh God, Jeff." He turned his head away violently and retched.

"Yeah, that was his name," Rat Face said. "He came here with you before. This time he tried to steal."

"Stupid," Chris said through his tears. "Why'd you come *back*?"

"Wait a minute," I said. "You didn't know he'd come back here?" Chris shook his head. It was all crowding in on him. He'd had a pretty hairy time. He was starting to shut it out—the body here, the faceless body in the mind, the hot blood still pumping in that brimstone darkness, this sweet, rotten smell, my questions. "I thought finding Jeff was what this was all about," I said.

He turned and walked back to the Harley. Jennifer gave him a questioning look and Happy walked over to touch his arm. He revved the engine and looked straight ahead. I retied Rat Face. "See that fucker gets it," she said.

She was from New England and it came out "fucka." "That fucka Lane." I thanked her and told my parade to move out. Maybe we could get clear of here before any more bodies showed up. Let the sheriff come for the rest of it.

We were slow. It wouldn't have mattered except that we had to pass through the Pseudo-Hoopa. I figured we'd make as much noise as possible and show them we'd captured their enemies and were marching them like slaves to Gancy. Chris revved the Harley. Happy fired his shotgun. I took the suppressor off the Uzi, put in a regular stick, and gave them a few bursts of Israeli martial music. When we reached the point where we'd seen the two men before, I stopped and yelled up into the trees: "It's all right. Look. We're taking them away."

Four Hoopa men and two women came out to mock the Midnight Miners. They wore only loincloths, but the women were dirty and ugly and did not inspire the sort of *National Geographic* lust I usually feel toward naked primitives—or at least the odorless ones in photos. They walked up and down our column, taunting and poking the men and women. When they started spitting, Happy told them to knock it off.

Then Chris surprised us again. He got off the Harley and disappeared into the woods from which the Hoopa had come. Happy started in after him, but I waved him off. "Give him a few minutes," I said.

It was a little longer than that before Chris came out of the pines leading a big, blonde woman who didn't seem to know where she was. She was now wearing Chris's T-shirt and a large loincloth improvised from an old bath towel. Chris's bare chest and arms had his old man's Popeye knobbiness.

Happy's mouth dropped open. One of the Hoopa men stirred a little, but the others held him back. Like real Indians, they admired courage and/or respected insanity. Chris led the woman up to Happy, who put his arms around her. She let him hold her. She raised her ragged head back—she was taller than Happy—and watched him cry against her for a few beats, as though there were something familiar about it. She looked at Chris standing beside her in the same distant way. Chris was crying, too. So was Jennifer. I was having a little trouble acting like a commando myself. Chris had found his mother.

"So this is why you came," I said to Jennifer. "To find his mother?" She nodded. I gave her some time to pull herself together.

"He saw her when he was here before," she said when she could. "When he and Jeff lived with those geeks. How weird is that, bugging out for the wilderness and accidentally finding your lost mom? We came back to get her out. We were watching the Indians from across the river, waiting to be sure she was there before we contacted them. Two of these geeks caught us."

Unbelievable. How weird was that, Jennifer wondered. In this case, just about average. Find something stranger than life.

"Did they . . . hurt you?" I asked her.

She wiped tears from her face with dirty hands. Sierra mascara. She looked more like a pioneer than a Valley Girl. "I stalled them," she said. "I told them I was engaged to marry a rich Columbian boy who expected me to be a virgin."

"That sounds like an aphrodisiac to these mutants."

"Well, they knew a little about Columbian revenge. I also told them my dad was in the CIA. He arranged the marriage. They kill us or send me back damaged, there isn't a country in the world where they're safe. Not from death. From worse. I was hoping they wouldn't get Mom on the phone. I don't think she could have played it tough."

"I took care of that. It worked? They left you alone?"

"Until now. They're always drunk or stoned. They're not very smart."

"You are. Nice work."

"Nice work yourself. Better than having a real dad in the CIA."

"Don't get mushy."

Leila was there at the fence to meet us. I kissed her until she complained of my odor. Then I sent her to call 911 and yell murder, et cetera. Send the paddy wagon, the EMS, the medical examiner, the homicide boys, the whole team. She said they'd found their cop snipers in the north. I kissed her again, then told her she'd better call Sarah right after she got the cops. We'd wait.

Actually, *I* waited. I suggested that Happy take the rental car and illegal weapons and drive the kids and his ex-wife into the hospital at San Luis Rey. Diane would need some very special care, but she'd waited so long that an extra hour in a car wouldn't make any difference, and then they'd all be closer to home. I'd stay behind to guard the Midnight Miners. I've had better company.

Twenty-five

We sat around the Foxes' dining room table. Sarah had flown out. The supper dishes were cleared, and there were several newspapers on the table. We had eclipsed the Kampground Killer. In fact, one editorial writer had suggested that the FBI hire us to catch him. We were very hot copy. One headline read: CAROLINA RESORT PI BUSTS MANSONITE NAPPERS. It even gave my address. I wondered if Verco Watkins knew he lived in a "posh playground." The sheriff hadn't found any faults with our operation, although I still expected to hear from agent Linville.

We weren't all there. Leila had flown back to write her story and work out her two weeks' notice at the *Times*. She would join me in Highlands after I'd driven back. She and Sarah had crossed paths and never met. Diane was at the Shasta Center. "And we didn't kill a soul," Happy said proudly. Chris smiled. Becky came up behind and hugged her father.

"We saw a bumper sticker on the way home," Happy said. "Tell 'em what it said, Chris."

"'Take your boy hunting instead of hunting for your boy,'" Chris said. We all laughed.

"You did both," I said, and added: "Teach your children well."

"It was Providence," Martha said. Even Sarah seemed to believe that. She had just come in from smoking in the yard. She and Happy were having fun, but that didn't make him friendly toward tobacco. Even Martha seemed relaxed, although both an ex-wife and a childhood sweetheart had popped up within a week. I'd given her the cross I bought from Petey Pollard. She gave me a surprisingly warm hug. It seemed to please Happy as much as her.

"I'm going to stay here," Jennifer took the occasion to announce. "Chris and I are getting married."

Sarah blanched. Happy joined her. I walked out to the garage. I hated scenes like this. I heard voices raised. I saw an old plastic paddle sticking out of a cardboard box full of swim fins, softballs, and obsolete toy cars. I yanked it out and took it inside.

I already had the gist of this argument. Happy and Sarah wanted them to wait until they finished high school. Jennifer was about to pitch one of her famous fits. Now that she was a heroine, it promised to be a killer. I handed Sarah the paddle. She turned even paler. Jennifer looked at me with disbelief, then a mood that I couldn't read, then a kind of relief and acceptance. She turned and walked into the kitchen.

I pointed my thumb in that direction. Finally Sarah got up and followed her daughter, like somebody on a date with a firing squad. Eventually, we heard a timid slap—on designer jeans—and a second, and a stronger third. Then we heard Jennifer's voice and Sarah's raised above it and three more sound whacks. Then, when we thought it was all over, we heard a final one, which seemed to have in it the full power of Sarah's dammed frustration.

Then she joined us. She looked years younger. She held the paddle the way a tennis ace holds his racket. Jennifer followed her out, wet eyed and relaxed. Jennifer shrugged at Chris and he shrugged back. I think he looked relieved, too. We all were. Sarah handed the paddle to Happy. Chris started for the kitchen. Happy shook his head no. Chris came over to hug his old man. Happy gave him the paddle to return to the garage.

That night the drought broke. It rained all night.

I lit out the next morning, driving like Neal Cassady's ghost, warping the miles. I should have been happier than I was. I got gas in Nevada, in a place that had a bar where everybody was drunk at ten o'clock Sunday morning. These are the "salt of the earth," down-home folks that Charles Kuralt doesn't show on the road on Sunday morning. Coming through Kansas, I heard a PBS interview about an essay in the *Hudson Review*, the gist of which was that we were eating the earth the way slime mold devours its environment, hoping to send up rockets and robots and silicon substitutes with our genetic message—the way the mold sends its spore towers and spits the next generation of slime into space—before it was too late. DNA is everything, someone said. The genetic imperative. Our bodies are only vehicles for our genes, and not very good ones at that.

The author described our loathing of the physical world and its limitations. He cited writing from Iranian mystics to Loren Eiseley to NASA engineers. "We hate our bodies," one said. "We hate the idea of dying. There has to be a better way." The piece was called "Departure of the Body Snatchers."

I'd read elsewhere that DNA fingerprinting was now a real part of crime detection. A microscopic trace of blood or semen or a few hair cells could yield a pattern distinct from millions of others. It was being used already in prosecutions. How much longer before we'd be checking DNA for the criminal tendency? Would we soon be screening and isolating people like the Kampground

Killer? And what kind of reading would I get?

I went into a Missouri Ho-Jo that turned out to be full of people just smoking and drinking coffee, with no non smoking section. It wouldn't have helped anyway. I used the men's room, figuring I could stand it that long. There was a guy in the crapper, one of those same old rednecks just sitting in there dumping his cigarette ashes on the tile floor as he smoked, fuck anybody who came along later. Why do they do that? Why did I do what I did?

I tucked a paper towel into the sprinkler on the ceiling. I saw his matches lying at the edge of the stall and reached under and took them. He only grunted again. "You're stinking up the place with that smoke," I said. "And dumping ashes on the floor." He only grunted again. I lit the paper towel. "That's O.K.," I said. "I'll clean it up for you."

I walked out and sat in my Eagle long enough to see the smokers' Ho-Jo conventioneers begin ducking and holding jackets and menus over their heads like folks caught in a summer shower as the sprinkler system washed the place down.

The Top 40 stations were still playing the Doors, although the hurricane season was over and the fires were out in the west. Lying in a Paris cemetery, Jim still had the hottest song in the US. We love our dead artists in this country.

In Tennessee I saw a place called Earl's Used Auto Parts and Racquetball Courts and knew I was back in the South. When I reached the Smokies, I saw that it had been a poor autumn. The leaves should have been brilliant by now, but they'd only had that one cold snap just about the time this case began. Unless they got another one soon, the leaf season would be a complete bust, and they'd just fall like dirty paper when winter came. The moon was building toward full. I thought this was the harvest moon—the fullest of the autumn—but I wasn't sure.

Nothing about this season had felt right. Maybe getting home would do it, and having Leila come. There was a slim chance she could already be there. She wasn't sure the paper would insist on her two weeks' notice, and if it didn't, she planned to do the writing there with me. I climbed that last dirt road in the Eagle and pulled in to my driveway, expecting to see Jack jumping at the end of his chain on the cable run I'd built from his house to my cabin.

My headlights showed no leaping husky, no Siberian mask and Gioconda black-gummed grin. Maybe Verco had him for some reason. I stopped and left the headlights on. I saw Jack's head in his doghouse door. He must be sick. The feeling I'd carried all these miles told me it was worse than that. And as I walked up to greet him, I smelled the smells I thought I'd left behind in the Midnight Mine camp.

His eyes were open in the harsh headlights, their surface dry and dead. I heard flies. I smelled old blood and new decay. I reached back for his collar to pull him from the house and his head came free with it. I reached back, gagging and choking—and crying—and grabbed the heavy fur of his shoulders and pulled the rest of him from the dog house. I held him in my lap and cried and remembered how I'd bought him ten years ago from a pet shop cage as a present to myself for getting sober. His situation had improved as mine had, although we had many of the same weaknesses and maybe didn't deserve to live so well. Now someone had butchered him to hurt me.

I went back to the car and strapped on the .45 and the knife. I unpacked the Uzi and slung it over my shoulder. Maybe whoever killed him was out there watching, but nothing was going to keep me from burying Jack. I got a spade from the utility barn and dug a grave near his house. I put him in it as naturally as I could. Now and then I could hear myself making strange noises through the beat of my own blood and the sounds of digging.

When I was finished, I rummaged through my packed rescue hardware and found the night goggles. I turned off the car headlights. If nobody had picked me off by now, chances were he wasn't there but was enjoying the probability of my sorrow at some safe distance. Or maybe it was my grief he wanted to see before he made a move. Whichever the case, I had the goggles and so—when I came to my senses a little—I used them.

I went into my house that way. My house was green and ghostly. Someone had broken in. The door was hanging open, almost torn from its hinges. Nobody kept much security up here. Few of us locked our doors unless we would be gone for a while. It hadn't been necessary to do all that damage to get in. It was part of the message. The rest was on my bed: parts of Jack that I hadn't missed earlier and a note that read: "I'm waiting for you."

Twenty-six

I knew where he'd be. I drove to the campground at the lake. The sign read closed. I couldn't figure out why it would be closed now unless they feared the Kampground Killer. Too late for that. I left my car and went around the chain. I had the Uzi, the .45, and the K-Bar. I was wearing the goggles. The campground showed signs of hasty departure. Maybe it wasn't the rangers who closed it. I could picture the guy I'd seen at the rest stop, dressed in one of James Dillard's Smokey the Bear shirts or even one of his wife, Josie's. Josie was a big girl. They'd gotten married last spring and ran the campground for the state.

I couldn't find anybody. I wandered back though the grounds until finally, at the remote end behind the lake, I saw a tent. I came up quietly, and heard the noises I'd first heard him make at that interstate rest stop. A woman's legs stuck out from under the flap. Were they familiar? They showed smudges and trails of blood, drying, turning brown.

But maybe she was alive. Maybe he had a gun under there. Maybe this was a trap. I couldn't see him handling James with a knife, and James was gone. That was the last real thinking I did. I shot away the tent stakes with the Uzi. I'd left the suppressor off and packed a regular magazine, and the noise was sudden and, I hoped, terrifying for him. The tent fell around his seated form and I heard, in that new silence, the same noises of passion. I needed to be sure it was he and not some other victim, so I put down the Uzi, pulled out the K-Bar, walked onto the collapsed tent, pulled the fabric up from his head and cut it away. When I had a good hole, I yanked it down over his head and shoulders.

It was my man, or maybe he was no longer a man. He looked different. He'd undergone a transformation into something like the shape of pure evil—not hairy and beastly and blood-engorged but sleek and slick and pale, as if *his* blood had been emptied here or had been replaced with something else. He looked like something that had rarely seen the light. His features, never distinctive, had withdrawn further—ears, nose, hair now close against the long, damp skull. In his eyes was not the flash of rage but the cold glare of eternal doom. Once, twice, like a superimposed film image or cutaway, I had a glimpse of what had been human, and it seemed eager, desperate, for me to finish my, our business. Maybe part of him was glad to see me, ready to pass his burden on to me. I understood what he needed and it was now the same that I needed, my need finally as powerful as his. I didn't want to touch him, but I cut him, my first a glancing blow which took his ear and then cut into his shoulder. I don't remember after that. *Your* blood, fucker. *You* die, *you* die, *you* die. I cut him everywhere. I heard his moans with my own.

I kept killing him long after his had stopped, no longer aware of having a weapon. His body seemed to melt under my assault until it was lying flat in the hacked tent fabric and lacked real definition. I dropped the knife and moved around to grab the girl's legs and pull her out. It wasn't Leila. It was Josie. The man I'd just killed was wearing her clothes.

Twenty-seven

I'd only killed those two guys in Atlanta, in self-defense and after going through what felt like death in me—death of my own courage, even my survival instinct—and coming out the other side. Most of us never come close; even Happy had avoided it. It made me an even bigger hero. The Kampground Killer had clubbed James with a pipe wrench as he stood at a urinal in the welcome center. Reassured that James was dead, he'd put him on a commode and closed the stall door. Then he'd lured Josie to his tent on some pretext and stabbed her. Then he'd put on her shirt and gone through to close the campground so he could return for a more leisurely visit. The Medical Examiner felt that he'd killed Jack first, then gone to the lake, to kill the Dillards and wait for me. Nobody could figure how he'd known I'd be back that day. Nobody ever did, exactly. A lot of our plans were in the papers. Maybe he made some phone calls, pretending to be a reporter.

Verco, Sr., had been in been in bed with the flu, and Verco, Jr., was in Chapel Hill doing research. Mrs. Watkins had a bad hip, and they figured Jack would be all right for a few days. It may have saved their lives. The killer wouldn't have had a problem getting close to Jack; I'd taken him for guard training, but although he didn't mind fighting other dogs, he liked people too much and the trainer said he was too old to learn different. The trainer recommended another breed, another dog. Maybe some day I would.

A former client of mine had a remodeled boat house on Bald Head Island, just south of Wilmington at the mouth of the Cape Fear River. It was an environmentally sensitive development, she said. I could stay there any time I wanted. This seemed a good time.

Leila joined me for a while. Her article was finished. There were no phones in the houses on Bald Head. Just CB radios. But after a couple of weeks, she went to the town hall and called the famous Boston magazine where she'd sent her piece. They offered to buy it and to give her a job.

"It's perfect," I said. I'd been running and swimming a lot, riding around through the coastal forest aimlessly in the electric golf carts they substitute on Bald Head for cars.

"Unless you want to get married and have kids before I'm too old," she said. She covered the serious offer with a grin.

I grinned back, unable to be serious about anything, running before my own interior storm. "It's too good a chance to pass up," I said.

"You're tired of living here anyway," she said. "You were going to move out west. Come to Boston instead. Start working Spenser's turf."

"Maybe I will," I said. "I need some time."

"They want me right away," she said. "I'll get a temporary place, wait until I hear from you." I took the boat with her to Southport and drove her to the Wilmington airport.

I got weirder for a while on the island. I tried to convince myself that Leila was ambitious, that she'd only been with me for the story. That would allow me to be alone and spare her what I feared was coming. I didn't know what it was I still feared. Maybe it was Leila.

Leila and the demons I'd loosed again back at the Campground. I'd had my kill, blooded myself, faced the great death back in Atlanta years ago. I'd killed two cracker thugs who'd kidnapped and intended to kill me. I thought that would take care of it. I'd never realized how happy I was with that blown knee until then. Now I was going through it all over again with a mass murderer. I'd wondered while the guys I trained with went to Southeast Asia and killed and died, feeling that I'd missed something, graduation maybe. I got to see how it felt, and now again, and it kept on feeling. Now I was clearly one of *those.* I'd paid the price of losing myself and now, like my boatmates, and in a phrase they sometimes used, I *knew* things. I'd *seen* shit. Now the ceremony of innocence was drowned, the blood-dimmed tide was loosed, and Yeats's rough beast was squirming inside me. My expectation had been that I'd be much less troubled if it ever had to happen again, and that wasn't quite true.

There weren't many of us there. I paid a fortune each night to eat in the only restaurant and finally, when I'd been the only customer for three nights running, got the *maitre* to turn off the Musak. After that I ate in silence, the waitress nervous without music and me feeling like a tyrant of some kind in my lonely dining hall.

I was afraid of the kitchen knives with Leila gone. There were six of them in a wooden block. At first I buried them outside. Then I feared someone could find them and use them, so I slept with them under the bed.

I got a wet suit, mask, and fins, and took to swimming in the Cape Fear current, which was illegal according to several signs. Sometimes it would sweep me out into the Atlantic and I'd have to drift and rest and try to come back around to strike the northern tip of the island, far from where I'd gone in.

Barry worried about me. He was the security guard with the iron-pumped arms. But then I was a national hero and former SEAL, and he could hardly tell me not to swim. The few people left out there got used to seeing me driving a golf cart in a wet suit, but the quality of their waves changed, and I thought that while Barry was worried about my safety, they might now be worried about their own.

One night I went down to the beach with the naturalist girl who looked after the loggerhead nests along the Atlantic side. We found a nest and a tiny, struggling straggler, about the size of my Rolex, who followed our light down to the beach with an unbelievable burst of energy and disappeared into the surf, where the turtle lady told me the odds were a thousand to one against his reaching maturity. Until he was grown, everything out there was his enemy: seabirds, fishes, boats, nets, humans. It seemed so hopeless.

The turtle lady was about Leila's age, but quiet and very private. She lived in a converted boat house on the other side of the island from me. I asked her if she wanted to swim. She said it was cold. I said so what. She said we didn't have suits. I said so what. We swam. We shivered. We tugged on our clothes over our wet bodies. We rode to her place and made love. It was salty and hungry and desperate. It was all about the turtle and how easy it is to die, and kill.

Then it turned cold and clear and I heard about a run of bluefish. I borrowed a surf rig and a big spoon and went down in my wet suit to the mouth of the Cape Fear. Bluefish are the salt-water piranha. When they're in a feeding frenzy, they'll hit anything. Fishermen have found human fingers inside them. They're big, strong, vicious, and—when quickly bled and gutted, with the dark, fishy flesh removed—delicious. I thought about the turtle. I hit into the run and caught bluefish until my arms trembled and they littered the beach. I killed them until I started to feel better. Then I packed them into a heavy duty trash bag and hauled them up to my place.

I set up some saw horses and a piece of plywood and filleted all thirty-seven of them. I don't know how many pounds of fish I had. Blood and fish guts were everywhere, and the gulls gathered. It got dark and started to rain, but I kept it up, eating raw pieces as I worked. I packed my freezer and then portioned out the fillets into family-sized plastic bags and stacked them on the porch.

I went in, washed, and called the turtle lady on the CB to invite her for supper. She came, in the covered Jeep they allowed her because she'd been there so long and needed it sometimes for her work. We cooked grits and tomatoes and she warmed up some cornbread from her last night's supper while I broiled bluefish. We ate like Vikings, like cannibals. She told me not to worry about the turtle, that his kind were among the oldest creatures still on earth. They had carried their DNA very successfully without rockets, robots, computers, or Uzis, and nowadays they got a little help from people like her. We made love again and she went home. I think she was a little scared of me. I was a little scared of me, too, but I left the knives where they were in the kitchen.

I put on some foul weather gear and went out into the storm that had been building all night. I rode around in my golf cart, delivering bluefish to everyone who had a light on. I had a lot left, so I found Barry and made him open the restaurant so I could put the rest into their freezer. It was important to me that the fish not go to waste. Barry went along. He still hadn't figured out what to say to me.

I stayed there another week and then went back to the mountains. It got cold enough for us to have a little more color in the leaves before they fell, but it had not been a normal autumn. After a while, though, I felt better. I'd been three weeks on the island and spent another week cleaning house in Highlands. That should be time enough for a man to find salvation.

About the author

Richard Hill is the author of an earlier novel, *Ghost Story*, and his writing has appeared in *Harper's, Esquire, Playboy, Omni, New Letters, The New York Times Book Review, Rolling Stone*, and numerous other publications. He has a Ph.D. from Florida State University, has worked as a carpenter and as a caretaker of a ranch on the wilderness side of Oregon's Rogue River, and has operated his own karate dojo. He has won an NEA Fellowship, an O. Henry Prize and a PEN/Algren citation, and was nominated by the US panel to be the first Raymond Chandler Fulbright Scholar to Oxford in mystery and espionage writing.

Mr. Hill now lives in Wilmington, North Carolina, where he teaches writing at the University of North Carolina. At present he is writing a screenplay about the life of karate master Joe Lewis, while working on the next "Gat" Sierra novel.